TWELVE
BELOW ZERO

Also by Anthony Bukoski and published by Southern Methodist University Press

Children of Strangers (1993)

Polonaise (1999)

Time Between Trains (2003)

North of the Port (2008)

TWELVE BELOW ZERO

STORIES BY ANTHONY BUKOSKI

NEW AND EXPANDED EDITION

HOLY COW! PRESS :: DULUTH, MINNESOTA :: 2008

Cover and text design by Clarity (Duluth, Minnesota).

Printed in Canada.

First printing, Fall, 2008.

10 9 8 7 6 5 4 3 2 1

The title story and seven others—revised for this edition—first appeared in *Twelve Below Zero* (New Rivers Press, 1986). "Stan and Ollie" and "Harry and the Dancer" are now called "The Sons of the Desert" and "Wesolewski, Hedwig Room 301," respectively. Of the new stories, "The Pulaski Guards" first appeared in *Southern Humanities Review*, where it won the Theodore Christian Hoepfner Award, and "Your Hit Parade" first appeared in *Chronicles: A Magazine of American Culture*. "Shovel Work" and "The Wood-Bat League" are also new to this edition.

The author is grateful to April Solberg for typing the manuscript on disk and to Janet Blair for helping him in matters large and small at the University of Wisconsin-Superior.

Library of Congress Cataloging-in-Publication Data
Bukoski, Anthony.
Twelve below zero : stories / by Anthony Bukoski. —New and expanded ed.
p. cm.
ISBN 978-0-9779458-7-0 (alk. paper)
I. Title
PS3552.U399T84 2008
813'.54—dc22 2008027628

This project is supported in part by grant awards from The Alan H. Zeppa Family Foundation, The Lenfestey Family Foundation, and by gifts from generous individual donors.

Holy Cow! Press books are distributed to the trade by:
Consortium Book Sales & Distribution, c/o Perseus Distribution,
1094 Flex Drive, Jackson, Tennessee 38301.

For personal inquiries, write to:
Holy Cow! Press, Post Office Box 3170, Mount Royal Station, Duluth, Minnesota 55803.
Please visit our website: www.holycowpress.org

For John Hanson,
who understands the North

CONTENTS

8
Preface by Barton Sutter

11
Twelve Below Zero

25
I, Miss Lillian

35
The Pulaski Guards

49
Shovel Work

67
Hello from Ture

85
The Sons of the Desert

91
The Wood-Bat League

103
Your Hit Parade

115
Wesolewski, Hedwig Room 301

127
Great Sea Battles

135
The Woman Who Ate Cat Food

145
Ice Days

157
Afterword

161
About the Author

PREFACE

SUPERIOR, WISCONSIN, is a long, long way from Los Angeles and New York, where American reputations tend to be made, which may explain why Anthony Bukoski still has not received the recognition he has earned. Although he's been honored by the Christopher Isherwood Foundation in California, although his work has been read at Symphony Space in New York, although his fiction is discussed in leading Polish journals, although he has an audience of delighted readers, the larger public has yet to learn what these people already know: that the inland port of Superior, Wisconsin, where Bukoski practices his craft, has produced one of the finest contemporary short story writers in the country.

The stories Bukoski writes are remarkably varied in kind: comedies that make you cry; tragedies that make you laugh; cartoons and vaudeville pieces; strange, dark allegories; and, the ones that move me most, deeply sympathetic portraits of ordinary people. Geographically, too, the tales may range as far as Louisiana, Poland, and Vietnam; yet even these are normally tied to Bukoski's primary source, the stark but lovely landscape of northern Minnesota and Wisconsin, populated by Native Americans, Swedes, Germans, Poles, and Finns.

The incandescent question that burns through almost all of Bukoski's stories is asked explicitly by a character in "Shovel Work": "Is it immoral to want something before one's time on earth is up?" The abyss between the grand, almost operatic yearning of Bukoski's characters and what they get, what they have to settle for, is heartbreaking. Desperate to please his dying grandmother, a young man joins the moribund Polish Club and bets big on a meat raffle. The reward for a lifetime of hard labor may turn out to be the taste of a windfall apple. Longing for connection, the people in Bukoski's fiction console themselves with the blues broadcast on KSAD radio or dial numbers scribbled on the walls of telephone booths or peep through keyholes. It's enough to make you weep...and weep you will, when you catch your breath from laughing.

Bukoski's supreme theme is heartache: the longing for history, culture, the Old Country, community, respect, and, above all else, requited love. Of this theme, he seems to me the undisputed modern master. He is Edward Hopper with a sense of humor. His dialogue sounds like Erik Satie. His passages on loneliness—rich, headlong arpeggios worthy of Chopin—make music out of heartache. The longing to belong, to love and be loved: *Is* there a greater theme?

So I am glad and more than glad—deeply pleased—to have this new and expanded version of *Twelve Below Zero*, the collection in which, many years ago now, Bukoski's stories first appeared. The early tales have been changed significantly by this ardent reviser, and the book includes four new stories: "The Pulaski Guards," a family romance; "Shovel Work," an extended gag about love and well-drilling; "The Wood-Bat League," a tribute to an old-style baseball park; and a real tour de force, "Your Hit Parade," in which a wee hours DJ, concerned for his Golden Age demographic group, sympathizes with their worries, croons nostalgic recollections of the old hometown, and confesses his regrets and sins by telling stories from his childhood, beaming his heartache out into the night, hoping it might help—not a bad metaphor for what that character's creator has been doing for the last few decades. Listen.

Barton Sutter

Twelve Below Zero

You can hear accordions playing at the End-of-the-Line Café. You can curse there, fight and cut or burn yourself for sport. You can sip blood soup and hawk and spit among the herring scales on the floor. Anything you want there is yours. You can smack your fists on the oaken bar or stand on one leg and howl and bark like some creature from Bad River or Cornucopia.

Men are tough at the End-of-the-Line. Some have lost toes and fingers to the frost. Others are missing arms or parts of hands. But no matter, they're strong. From time to time, outsiders try to prove otherwise. One I recall was six feet four. He wasn't so big the boys couldn't take care of him. He was a loudmouth from Blueberry, a whistlestop near Two Heart, which lies fifty miles east of Superior. Taking a wallop to the stomach, the big shot fell to the floor in front of Harry LeCroix, the meanest one in here. That's how hard the whistlestop loudmouth was hit, or how drunk he was—I forget which. Harry wouldn't let him stand up. On his hands and knees, the loudmouth had to make it to the door, had to crawl, not walk, through the spit and herring scales to the door.

Let me tell you more about the End-of-the-Line Café. One patron was a sawyer, Augie Benner. Another was Thomas Thorsen.

They were so unlike each other, so completely different, that I don't see how they could have done what they did. In addition to Harry LeCroix, Augie, Thomas Thorsen, and the other trappers, loggers, and Great Northern railroad hands, there were these lovely patrons: Betty Blaine and the seven or eight women who hang around.

And I? After workdays bringing the mail to houses and businesses in this area of Douglas County, I spend nights reading. I am the only one in the End-of-the-Line who does this. If the men in the tavern knew I was a solitary reader, a forty-eight-year-old who thinks about life and has read a thousand books, they'd make me crawl like the braggart from Blueberry. But the sawyer, Augie, won't tell. And I have sworn to keep Betty Blaine's secret from others if she doesn't tell that I study at night. So I guess I'm safe when I come in the End-of-the-Line for an hour, and that no one knows I'm writing this. It's not good to get smart or to think you know more than others. They'll hear if you've gotten wise on them or taken a correspondence course or studied under the glow of the kitchen lamp with Miss Pesark. They will mistreat you, and you might end up being hurt.

In the End-of-the-Line, a tragedy occurred to two men because they were out of the ordinary. As the story goes, Mr. Edward Nelson, the café's owner, had hired Thomas Thorsen to protect his interests. What a figure he made. Tall, straight-backed, handsome, he had curly hair, bright blue eyes, a bull-like neck, hammers for fists. He was strong and delicate at the same time, a character like I've read about in literature, "a superb figure tossed up as by the horns of Taurus against the thunderous sky." If he could move away from here to Superior or Duluth, I saw possibilities for Thomas Thorsen. The regulars teased him about being young. They liked him. Coming into the dim, hot End-of-the-Line, he was a breath of fresh air eager to protect you if you didn't cause trouble. It's something for a youngster to be respected by hard drinkers, laborers, and violent men. He was a star around here, like Alan Ladd or Tyrone Power.

Before coming to work at the End-of-the-Line, Thomas Thorsen, movie star, had delivered wood to Two Heart businesses in a beat-up truck. From all the woodchopping and lifting, his arms and chest were big. The time he spent in the woods hunting increased his lung capacity. In the tilt of his head, in the way he rose from the tables that ring the long walls, I saw a sensitive twenty-four-year-old, not a brawler, gouger, and biter. Finishing their drinks, tossing their cigarettes on the floor, most patrons stand up as though they own the place after six or eight hours in here. Before Thomas Thorsen rose from a chair, he nodded to this one, winked at that one, shook another man's hand. Checking to see whether he had his rings on straight, he gathered his spare change and the gifts Nelson had given him. Am I imagining the patient, delicate thoughtfulness of Thomas Thorsen?

I noticed it at the interview when Nelson convinced him to try the bar business. "If you don't help me, the place will be hard for me to keep. The business will go under for sure. Somebody will do something awful in here. That'll be it," he said. When Thomas Thorsen hesitated in order to sip his beer, the boss, knowing he was fighting for his future, offered him more money. He promised him a coat and new boots and gloves. The young man was curling a lock of hair about his finger when he agreed to sign on.

"When is spring coming?" he asked me the first day he kept the place safe from the wildmen the north wind blew his way. When? A good question. The solid rings on his right hand could damage a man's forehead or dent his face if Thorsen had to fight his way to springtime.

Straight off, he tussled with a dairy farmer from Oulu who'd broken a whiskey bottle on the sidewalk and threatened to grind Nelson's face in the glass. When the dairyman refused to leave the premises, Tom took off part of the man's nose in the fight. "Get out on the street away from here. At least don't stand in the doorway, then we won't have to do this," Tom warned him. Some guys couldn't get it through their heads that finally Mr. Nelson was cleaning the place up, that they were the ones who'd reached the end-of-the-line with him. Thomas Thorsen took on two brothers. He broke their fingers with an axe handle. Another time he bloodied noses and blackened eyes with his fists, elbows, and rings. But the roughhousing having taken its toll, he was ready to quit after a month.

"Why don't you come home with me?" I asked him. Believing he was a sensitive youth, I wasn't as quiet with him as with others. "I'll find you work. I'll tell you about the people that live in Milwaukee and St. Paul. I'm different. I'm not like anyone," I confessed. Though I told him little more, afterward he wouldn't acknowledge me when I brought the mail to his mother or saw him on the street. Nevertheless, I thought the tilt of his head when I'd talked about St. Paul and other big cities indicated he was interested in what I had to offer. I guess he was thinking about the life outside of Two Heart, but he didn't want to let on.

If he lives as I do, he'll be isolated here, sure enough. No one will feel comfortable around him, I thought. Perhaps it frightens him knowing he could lose his youth, his popularity. When I think about him nowadays, I realize I myself could never have been young. In the winter twilight in back of the mail office, I have observed my reflection in the window glass—the receding hairline, the white hair at the temples, the forehead lined with worry, the high cheekbones, the hollow face of the philosopher of winter. I am six feet tall. From exerting myself on the mail route, I weigh 172 pounds. I am hunched from carrying mail into fierce winds. For thirty-five of forty-eight years, I've stayed to myself. I sit in the End-of-the-Line alone observing others.

When Thomas Thorsen wouldn't talk to me again, I thought perhaps I was wrong to have considered him a youth with potential, also someone I could tell about myself. I learned there was a woman interested in him. When he was supposed to be protecting Nelson's business, the boss would find him in back sitting on a beer keg dreaming about her. If you can imagine a wedding photograph of him and Betty Blaine, you would see Tom with his hair parted, his blue eyes sparkling, his face bright and happy, and Betty at his side, earnest and pretty. But there is no photograph. Now comes the wintery part, now the Augie Benner section. If you'll stay with me while I complete the last part of the triangle of Tom, Betty Blaine, and lonesome Augie Benner, I can get on with the story.

Augie was a sawyer, as I say. The ice, the winds, the frozen earth hadn't inclined him to violence the way it does others. He'd never fought anyone. Even so, Nelson did not like him, but for the sake of business, he would sidle over, inquire about Augie's day, and serve him a bowl of soup and bread and a cup of coffee.

Sometimes Augie's skin was so pale it seemed to me he was ready to die—unearthly it was. Patches of hair like steam stuck out from under the green-visored cap with earlaps. The expression of his face was gloomy—white hair over a colorless face. Occasionally, he pulled his ear, twitched an eyebrow, or did some strange thing he probably didn't notice he was doing. But the men noticed. It was as if his old clothes and his steam-white hair were a sign of some failing at the heart's core. He'd heard that children complained of catching his scent, that women were afraid to be touched by Augie's lonesome hands. People edged away from him, partly because of his looks, partly because of the smell, which I will explain. Every now and again someone comes in who smells as though he's worked in the fisheries or in the Poplar cannery and has neither bathed recently nor changed clothes. Even loggers, bartenders, and railroad men hold their breath when a person like him arrives and they are no longer free to breathe the northern air.

How do I explain Augie? No northern wanderer, he was a town citizen who held steady work at the sawmill. Maybe the snow or the wind whistling at midnight through the ice caves on the river made him what he was. The earth will turn against the ill-prepared. When it's twelve below zero, there is little hope for a friendless man. Malevolence falls with the snow. The leaden sky, the gray trees, the brittle earth haunt the person no one likes. He can't help the way he was born or how he has suffered in his youth, thus becoming what he is. When toasts were raised on snowy nights in the End-of-the-Line, no one lifted a glass to Augie. When everyone brought potatoes, venison, and bread for the booya at the café, no one invited Augie, who showed up after dinner was over. If this is difficult to believe, accept it as a metaphor.

For so long he had been acting strangely. He'd become a nuisance. Enough years of being treated this way and then what? I guess he was delighted with himself and the role he'd played for most of his life. What else could he do but be satisfied with himself? Finally, the smell and the way he acted got bad enough the patrons of the End-of-the-Line ordered him to wear a bell.

I watched the sentencing of Augie Benner through the tattered drapes separating the backroom from the café. These drapes have red and pink peony decorations. Four men sat at a table behind the draperies; other rough men lined the walls of the small room when they brought Augie in. "You're worthless. You make us gag," they said. "Open the window," someone said.

Augie had missing teeth and a growth on his lip. If he bit it again, it looked as though it would burst.

"I'm invited in?" he asked, curious to see what was going on.

"Invited?" said Harry LeCroix. "I wouldn't put it that way."

"Do you want to know what I have to say for myself?" Augie asked.

"What?" asked Harry LeCroix.

Though none of this made sense, Augie was trying to defend himself for once. "Am I invited in?" he asked again, but when they told him why he was with them behind the pretty draperies of the End-of-the-Line Café, he only managed to say, "Bless you, one and all" before they shoved him out. More men—he never saw who—shoved him to the café door.

From then on coming down Main Street or walking up behind someone, he was to ring the copper bell hanging from his neck. In that way, he would announce himself, so that no one would come near him. Once they'd done this to him, day after day he faded into his mackinaw, so that a person had to examine the shadow between cap, coat, and copper bell and whisper, "Augie, is it really you so frail and sickly?" Every night despite the condition of his health, he stopped in the café for soup or stew and a cup of coffee. This is where he heard of Tom and Betty Blaine. He was way down at the other end, where we made him sit alone, when he heard of their good fortune in love.

It was a blue night hovering around twelve below zero. He hated the long walk home. It was deep in the woods to Augie's place. Every spring when the daffodils bloom up here, people remember the sailor who'd sought the friendship of others. You hear how he fell asleep beneath the ice-glazed trees near Herbster; how, with the snow for a blanket, he closed his eyes, and the wind told him there is no friendship; and how he slept for months before anyone found him. When they did, dandelion and buttercup sprouted through the hood of his mackinaw, so that in the light, pleasing breeze, they were rubbing his thawing nose. He'd been frozen out. That's what'd happened.

Augie hated long hikes on starless nights when the ghosts of the dead are about. A little later he heard Thomas Thorsen telling Mr. Edward Nelson that he wouldn't go out to fight anymore, that there'd be no more dairymen from Oulu in his future. But Nelson surprised us.

"Why fight?" Mr. Nelson said. "There's no more reason to. The End-of-the-Line, thanks to you, is cleaned up. No more fighting, boys!" You could see Nelson was overjoyed. "We're throwing a dance on the eve of the full moon because of your work, Tom! For you and Betty, your sweetheart, it'll be whiskey, bread, and cake on the night the moon turns yellow on the horizon."

Nelson invited all of us to come. He asked Augie, "Say, why not join us? You can help serve cake if you like." The request worked salt into his wounds. The sawyer knew Nelson didn't mean it. It was no time to talk of cake when it was cold and he had to get home through the woods.

He hated the weather. He hated his white hair, especially when he was younger than some of the men. It was wrong what people did to him all those years. I can't say I liked him. But in this cold I can't stop thinking about him either.

Betty Blaine and another woman came in that night we were laughing at Augie. When the two women started in on him, he wouldn't take a refill on his coffee. He wouldn't look around, just sat staring at the calendar that read: January 1950. HOLSUM STRING CHEESE. EINO SAYS, "TRY IT, YOU'LL LIKE IT." Augie'd promised himself about drinking. In a severe country where winds set men thinking ill of others, such a thing is hard to avoid, especially when there's not much to do after work. Augie'd never had a woman as far as we knew. He had a home that was too far in the woods to wander home to easily.

There would be dancing and cake. Augie told me he'd never danced. In the café, the guys were laughing. Thomas Thorsen played the accordion and smiled at his bride-to-be. Thirty people clapped time. No one remembered Augie's reaching for the whiskey. No one cared—surely I didn't. That night of twelve below zero, Augie began to hate his condition. And no one, we found, could hate himself like Augie, the sawyer.

Alone at the other end of the bar, he started doing something, but his steps were off. No sooner had he set down the bottle than he'd begun this dance. The way he was shaking, it looked like St. Vitus' dance. He needed no music. When the people stared, he didn't let up. He was braying, spitting, twisting his body as the bell about his neck rang, and his head followed a few beats behind. Jerking his knees, swinging his arms in a rotary fashion, he began to laugh and sing in Swedish, *"Fader vår som är i himmeln."*

I was among those urging him on. How easy for an outsider like myself to want to be a part of something. I hate the way they spun him round, the way they grabbed his shirt and pulled him round and made him thrust his head through a bushel basket. It looked like he had a russet-colored skirt over his shoulders. When they threw pennies on the floor, he reached for them and the men kicked him. The bell rang ten times in succession. As he danced, spit flew from his mouth. The hair flapping up and down on the side of his head, the bell ringing, he must have wondered, as he danced, why he'd come so far north in the first place, why he'd left Trempealeau, Wisconsin, when he was Thorsen's age.

With everyone laughing, he asked what he was doing here. It was so funny. His arms high, head bobbing out of time, bushel basket sliding back and forth, the bell tolling requiem, he saw someone coming toward him, reaching out to him. To dance a schottische? To waltz him from the old, dark north? Pulling the basket off to dance with Thorsen, he hugged the boy gently and kissed him full on the mouth for the longest time.

After this, there are no photographs of Thomas Thorsen, neither with an accordion nor with the child his wife bore him. For all I know, he may never have had a photo taken again. He also threw the mirror out of his house. This much I'd heard: he couldn't stand to see his face. After returning Augie's kiss, he'd fallen to the floor as the sawyer hurried home through the woods.

Augie returned the next day looking for the boy. But, ashamed of what he'd done in the End-of-the-Line, Thomas Thorsen was gone. What fighter kisses an outcast? The men would hate him. If it had been Alan Ladd who Thorsen had kissed, then it wouldn't have been so bad. I know Thorsen avoided the sawmill where lonesome Augie worked.

Augie was fearful of what would happen to him next, too. At odd times he sneaked into the backroom of the café, where he asked Edward Nelson about the meaning of love. "Men love women," Nelson explained to Augie. "Don't you know that is the rule?" Still, no matter the snow, the wind, or the howling of beasts, Augie came to the End-of-the-Line. Nelson told him nothing more than the Rule of Man and Woman.

This is what's terrible in Augie's story; how sunrises came and noons and nightfalls, and how for his troubles he saw the river freeze deeper and the wolves deride the moon outside his door. Back he came looking for Tom. He was like the Herbster sailor needing to talk to someone or to just plain kiss someone before he froze and was discovered after five months of winter. Nelson could tell him nothing about Thomas Thorsen, though I told Augie that things have hidden meanings beyond our understanding and beyond the Man-Woman Rule. A person accepts the fact and goes on about the day's business, careful in the cold to protect himself. This wasn't enough for Augie.

"Tell me about him, please," Augie would say. And Nelson would answer, "I can't tell you. I don't know where he is these days." Then Nelson would close the door at the End-of-the-Line. As Augie said "Bless you, one and all," the customers shuffled around, coughed uncomfortably. Nelson told him he didn't know where Tom was because he didn't. I didn't either. Had Tom gone back to following the Rule? So much is inexplicable about a man's conduct, about Augie's conduct. You think you can examine and explain it. But in the process, and in spite of what you tell yourself you've found, you know you've come up empty. It's like winds blowing over snow; the patterns they make are hard to decipher.

I am a man who knows the place he lives in. I've suffered through its tragedies. If an outsider doesn't want to follow the Rule, he is crazy coming here if he can go elsewhere. After the kiss, Augie lived even more at the mercy of others. Surrounded by lakes, one as deep as the next, he and the rest of us were trapped. Augie would never get away from Two Heart, not with someone abroad in the night spying on him. When he was out, this stalker broke into Augie's cabin, which tormented his thoughts. The white-haired man with the bell didn't know what was happening, as if something bred in the mystery of darkness and the heart had made the north country frantic—and him desperate and miserable for love. Lakes, forest, and sky conspired against him. I guess he was giving up for the wind to scatter his ashes.

He wore rags. The bell clanged. Sometimes I thought it would strangle him. There were moments when he had to hide in the woods, hands over his ears, to avoid what they were saying in town. But their words echoed in the trees. The words came with the wind. The snow brought the words. "Did you see what they did—the two men? Did you see it?" The talk never ended.

Betty Blaine stopped by my house late one night. I forgot to say she'd married Thomas Thorsen in spite of Augie's kiss. What rankled her was the sullying of her husband's reputation. "Does he like Augie Benner?" people asked in whispers. Betty almost looked older than Augie. Her eyes had grown sunken and dark. Wrinkles appeared in her brow. She blushed at few things. Until one night she sought me like a charm. Augie Benner used to do that. It wasn't for advice Betty came, but for support in what she'd planned to do once she couldn't take the whispers anymore. That didn't take long.

Now I have to tell the story alone. There is no Augie. The terrorizing of this man had gone on for months. At first, Betty said nothing about it, nor even why she'd come to me, a man she hardly knew. Perhaps she thought I would tell her what I have learned in books. I don't know my own mind well. How could I tell her what was right for her to do? But I listened to her and was cursed. Before, I was innocent. I didn't know her story and was free of the guilt of knowing. Now, having listened, I knew. I had knowledge. She wanted to hear what I thought. "Do you know how I have been hurt because of that sawyer's actions?" she asked me. Simple enough, but not so simple.

She came again another morning. There was enough light to see through the woods. My windows were frozen over but the wind stopped blowing, and I could see her outline. She pounded on the door. Pushing it open, she walked to the fire, hair matted from the wool cap, eyes wild, dark.

A snow witch, she came a third time, a fourth. She came tapping on the windows, and I saw snow on her brow, ice dangling from her coat, frost on her fingers when she removed her heavy gloves.

Then a fifth time. It was morning. She said how she'd stalked the sawyer; how he'd bled and crawled and said something terrible about love; how he'd kept repeating the terrible thing to her; and how she'd tracked him for as far as he could go and how he put up no resistance. "You can find the trail. There's no sawyer. He's a red scar on the face of the earth," she said. "Go and find the trail and the bell yourself."

After that she left. "I don't need your fire," she said. I blocked my ears too late from the sound of her voice and what she was telling me. Who am I to tell? I am no longer innocent of knowing. I know more than the others except Betty, and she doesn't care about her knowledge so she's free of its burden. That's how knowing works. It's a burden unless you don't care. I have read too much with Miss Pesark not to care. I have studied Schopenhauer and Kant, the Germans; Kierkegaard, the Dane. I know about lonesome Augie what no one but Betty knows—how he died.

Following the red path, I found the place where Augie and Tom's wife recently disturbed the peace. A crust of snow had formed around him. To get to the bell, I removed his hat. His white hair blew in the wind, and I covered him with snow and let him sleep. Except for in the west, the sun was out. If you looked again, it was behind the snow. I've seen it snow for days. With no wind blowing, what is the difference if it snows? The wind started up that day. It was difficult finding my way back, the copper bell about my neck. I was lost in the metaphor of Augie Benner.

Thomas Thorsen, following the Rule now, is working again. Betty's resting at home expecting a child. Free to go to other interests, they are absolved, avenged, well-rested. She did what she set out to do, avenged herself and Thomas Thorsen. Everyone is working, resting, and law-abiding. But I have to tell the story of the killing of Augie Benner or go mad in the silence of my room. As far as Betty and the others, they're done with it, while I'm left thinking of Augie and of the Herbster sailor's story that once made the rounds—of how he was discovered thawing in the spring grass.

And what if, this frigid night, I meet bloody Augie on the pathway into town without having told his story? And what if he touches me with the fearsome touch? He tried telling someone what he felt, and look what it got him. I don't want to end up speechless within sight of town and with dandelions and buttercup in my hair next summer. Or to be blown about in strange ways like the twigs on the snow. Or kissed by someone known to be an outsider. But what then? Why, I wonder, should I, who for his own protection must pretend he can't read and write, be burdened with this secret and be the curst of God? I can't stop thinking that it's unfair I should have to wear the bell meant for another. People hear it ring. They talk about the wearer, about rules of behavior I cannot follow.

I am tired. I pace my room, stare at the fireplace, think about what I wish I didn't know—things about life, about Betty, about Augie Benner and the meaning of love. "Did you see what they did, two men in the bar?" people ask around. Sometimes, when I hear this, I have to go away fast to where the snow sifts through the pines, barely settling on the fur of the whitetail; to where the wind can't get at me if I hide my head deep in my hands to muffle the sounds of what they're saying about me in town. Tonight the forest is too loud for that, though. Practically every night there have been such rumors howling in the woods that I haven't been going out much.

I, Miss Lillian

"Before you leave, let me take your photo for the keepsake album," I beg the boy, Arvid. In the viewfinder of the box camera, I, Lillian Selwig, owner of the Blue Bell Hotel, capture him—worried look on his face—standing before the stone chimney. I want his photograph so I can remember how life was before Big Sammy turned against me, threatening to return in the middle of the night to harm us. The boy tells me he must leave me at the mercy of the winds. So be it. Before then I want his photo.

"Stand still pretending you're running your hand through your hair. Don't move," I tell him.

"It's hard standing this long in one place," he says.

"That's the nature of youth not to be content. But this last picture is important to remember you by—"

"Hurry before Sammy sees us," he says.

Six months ago Arvid never hurried. When we heard him in the room playing "Johann Pa Snippen," a song of our Swedish forefathers, he would stop as if to relax or to get a glass of water, then start playing again. The longer he stayed here—the first time, a one-day visit; the second time, a two-day visit; the third time, a week—the better he got along with the girls of the Blue Bell. Some of them were Swedes, the others Norwegians and Finns. He captivated them with his music. They captivated him with their poses and their lilac scents. Everything was lilacs when he came in May. We kept bouquets in rooms, on tables, even in the empty whiskey bottles lining the way to the river. He was especially attracted to one lilac-scented girl. Maarit wasn't the prettiest of the fifteen I employed, yet out of all of them, she got him up dancing. While others failed with lively songs played on the mandolin or tender songs sung softly to the night, she kept him twirling and spinning till bedtime.

To live here, you have to believe in the miracles of frost, music, and frozen, hidden things. Let me tell you something about this dreamer, Arvid. During his visits, he watched the goings-on but never took a woman to his room. Something else: he should have been named Orpheus, for he was forever tuning an ebony flute—an odd conjunction: the boy, the melodies, the snowy woods. When Maarit was with him, you could see her lose track of time she was so happy. But he seemed to care only for his music. You could hear the flute song on the lilac breezes of May, on the howling, blizzard winds of November. Compared to Big Sammy's looks and build, Arvid's thin arms, ripe lips, and blue eyes were as precious as music to Maarit and me. Youthful, beautiful assets—twenty-year-old assets such as he had—must be guarded from vicious people. Arvid needed someone sensitive like Maarit to protect him. But the flute he carried got in the way of things she wanted.

I, Miss Lillian, watched him wandering the summer woods and gardens, catching the falling October leaves, or climbing the high drifts on St. Lucia's Feast to look out at the distances to the south. By the time he borrowed my box camera, it was late December. As I spied on him spying on Maarit, he snapped her photo. When she left, I watched him steal her bracelets and wire earrings from the box she'd hidden beneath an icy stone. She was childish in this way, hiding trinkets in hillsides and along riverbanks. Later, he pretended he was the innocent, wandering flute player again. From the moment they learned from me of his thieving, the women in my place—old and young—vowed to help Maarit get him back for it. A thief is free to come to the Blue Bell Hotel where all are thieves of one sort or another—thieves of virginity, thieves of the emotions—but a chaste thief is not welcome. Our business has nothing to do with chastity, modesty, or celibacy. You priests stay away. You Lutheran moralizers stay away. You Baptist, bible-quoting hollerers—this is no place for you to take a room. We're sinners. We give you what you want. If you don't know what that is, we help you decide. We have Nora, the blonde-haired; Mona, the double-jointed; Cilla, the older woman; and Maarit if you like them young.

When Big Sammy and some of the camp's hangers-on caught Arvid wearing Maarit's trinkets beneath his sweater, they wagered how long it would take Maarit to make him hers. He was a northern wanderer, musician, thief, all of these things, but he'd never made love to a woman. This was the place to start at, in one of my clean, inexpensive rooms, each stocked with a bottle of whiskey and a washtub for your warm bath.

"He won't be a boy two nights from now," they said on January first.

"He won't last this night. He'll be hers by morning," they said on January third.

Betting fever took the place over. What else is there to do when the cold sets in? In the Blue Bell, we bet on everything—on the depth of the snow along the river, on who can walk on snowshoes to Pigeon Falls, on which owl we'll see first, the Great Grey or the Snowy, next winter. I wanted to show Arvid my body just as any woman here would, but I had to watch out, for Big Sammy had something up his sleeve when he observed the handsome boy. That's how trouble began: Sammy told me he'd bring someone in to help with the seduction of the thief. I did not hate Sammy then as much as I would come to hate him in a month.

"Do you remember Julija Debroux, the old woman?" he'd asked me. "Last summer's moss hangs on her skirts. I saw her on the road by the Temperance River. She was bringing her music to Kendall's camp."

To repay an ancient favor, he'd invited Julija Debroux to my place to earn a week's pay. She and the boy on whom Sammy wanted to bet were musicians; the boy with the flute, she with the gypsy fiddle. Sammy hoped they'd appreciate each other. He needed Julija to be confidential about the precise moment, the exact second, the boy fell for Maarit's charms. If Sammy had intimate knowledge of him and no one else but Julija and Maarit, of course, knew it, then there was no telling how much Sammy could win betting on a winter evening. Such is the power of music.

The crone, the hag, would provide an insurance policy for Sammy. She could give him the facts about Maarit and the boy. Because he's a tyrant, Sammy must never lose a bet. When he's happy we're happy, but cross him and he'll hurt you. The few times he's had to make good on a gambling bet, the Blue Bell shook with his rage. A huge man with red eyebrows and red tufts of hair on his knuckles and chest, I've seen him raise an axe and seven strokes later have enough wood for the night's fire. Once, he slapped a man so hard his ears rang for six months. Another time he made me strap a catalogue to my chest in order to shoot (yes, believe me!), to shoot his .22 rifle at the words MONTGOMERY WARD 1938. His bullets got to page twenty-five, Men's Underwear. I prayed the visitor was the answer and godmother to all of Sammy's fortunes.

So one night the old lady arrived during a storm. When I saw her, I remembered the thick, gray hair, the irises looking black in the firelight, the face casting shadows whichever way she stared. When she removed her coat and scarves and shook the chill from her bones, her cough startled me. I wondered how she could live with the thing in her lungs that was drowning her. Perhaps she'd already drowned years before and, snagged by a tree fallen in the river during ice breakup, had been magically restored to life. Sammy nursed her with drinks and soup. After an hour by the fire, she pursed her aged lips and hugged the fiddle to her chin. I was certain the boy would burst from excitement when he pressed close while the girls about him sang and danced.

Peculiar affections grow this deep in the woods. The flute player was enamored of the old woman's music. He was so given over to her that the following morning he wasn't happy until he'd heard a song from Julija's fiddle. All day he was entranced. And recalling what Sammy had asked (Sammy *demanded*, never asked), Julija directed the boy's attention to Maarit as she washed her hair or, naked, cut butterfly strokes with her arms through the steam in the bath. "There, that's the one for you," she said and pointed to Maarit. "Go on. Kiss her." After saying this, after coughing her lungs clear, she'd whisper to my Sammy, "I have the facts on them. I know it won't be long and they'll be—" She slipped the first rough finger of her hand through the circle made by her other hand.

Big Sammy was never happier than when it looked as though he'd won a bet. "It's clear that in one night the fiddler has bewitched him!" he said. Sammy bragged how the boy's entrance into manhood with Maarit was a mere formality now. He slapped his men on the back. He ordered the girl doing our cooking to bring sausages, cheese, and coarse, dark bread. But I, the keeper of the Blue Bell, he bullied because I didn't share his joy. What could I do against a man so powerful? I hated Big Sammy who fed me dry bread, then pushed me into the corner when the musicians' music filled his crazy head.

But one night through the frosted window I saw the boy with a light in his hand staring at me, at me when he could have had Maarit or Lulu. Arvid tapped twice, signaled, and held a rain slicker and a bearskin around me as he walked me through the cold to the small barn where we keep the summer's yard ornaments—the stone fountains the girls like, the statuary. On the way, I let him put his fingers around my arm. He did this gently. He reassured me. I let him touch my face. The tenderness he showed me is seldom seen here. Soon we were out of the snow and wind.

"Will you sit with me in the dry straw?" he whispered. Sammy was gone for the night. Arvid had to draw me to him I was trembling so. He helped me with my heavy coat, covered me with a blanket.

"What are you doing?" I asked, surprised, happy. I don't recall what he replied. We worried about Sammy, then stopped worrying when nothing mattered but the boy and me. His lips brushed my hands and wrists. I kissed him.

I wore a wool skirt, a blue shift, and heavy clothes under them. He wanted to undress me and warm me. "I played for you all those times," he confessed.

"Why?"

"Hush!"

Thinking we heard Julija, we lay quiet a moment. What he did when I kissed his neck took hardly longer than that minute. When he was done with it—the first time in his life!—I was disappointed and not disappointed. He was as innocent as we'd believed. I couldn't leave him. "You'd better go though," I said finally. Midnight having passed, the boy sneaking out with my blessing, I stayed there with the gray statues and fountains of the summer.

The next morning, Sammy, hungover, found me asleep. I pretended not to know why he was angry. "I came here alone," I said.

"You don't wear that kind of boot, Lillian. Whose tracks are in the snow outside the door?" Bull-like, flexing, he paced the floor, stood before me, his terrible majesty so different from the boy's quiet calm. I snapped his picture just as he twirled a cane chair from the summer garden and smashed it to the floor.

In the gray dawn, he asked the girls if *they'd* led me to the barn. "Had I been drunk and insulting them? Is that why they'd gotten me out of the hotel last night?" he'd asked. Not for two or three hours would he inquire this of the men. Distracted, he marched them outside to try their boots in the mysterious tracks. When one's boots were too small, he signaled another to step forward. He cursed them: this man's and that man's boots were small, wide, narrow, never the true fit. The true fit was reserved for the boy and me. All this time he remained upstairs with Maarit. Who knows what they were up to?

Among the whores and hangers-on, Arvid was the one person Sammy trusted. So much so that when the flute player appeared arm in arm with Maarit, my husband yelled, "See now where he comes from? Maarit's room! My time was closest! I bet it would be last night that he fell, didn't I? Wasn't I right? Do you see I was right?" But there was something missing—the joy one would expect to hear in a lucky man's voice. By then Big Sammy must have been aware that someone had also known the flesh of his aging woman, my flesh, Miss Lillian Selwig's.

Not thinking, I suppose, that the boy was the thief of my affections, Sammy called him to his side. Promising him a share of the profits made from the bet, Big Sammy hugged him for never lying as the others did. Before them, the camp's hangers-on filed past, the boy examining their boots. He came up with nothing incriminating (how could he, the bootprints were his?). The boy said, "These loggers, they're innocent. Their boots don't fit here, Sammy." At which time, assuming Sammy's anger would pass, the men dug into their pockets and threw down money in the snow, a peace offering.

"Let's have a party, Big Sammy," they said as they stood around the money pile. They tried to cheer him up. But no matter how Julija's music filled the air nor how the men urged him, he wouldn't budge onto the dance floor of the Blue Bell. Sammy wouldn't dance the two-step. He'd never been a dancing man. So they'd leave him alone, he sent someone to dance in his stead. When I saw the precious flute player waltzing toward me, asking would I like to dance with him in place of Sammy, I smiled and accepted with Sammy's permission.

Logger upon logger cut in after that, Eddie Mitchell, Sever Lunde, and all that time Sammy slouched in the corner fingering his tin of Red Man. No one failed to court me that day. For once, I, Miss Lillian, was the only woman in the place who counted. If it would have kept on like this, if it only could have kept on.

Yet, soon after, when Big Sammy talked of burning down the place, the boy slipped off into the forest. It was just as well. The possibility of my cheating on Big Sammy in my amours reduced him to madness. There was no telling who his fists would thrash at such times. The others circled him, asking in the nicest voices, "What's the matter with you all of a sudden, Sammy?" But he wouldn't answer. "Get away!" he hollered. He had a nervous habit of shaking his fists and falling to one knee when he was riled. So kneeling, he appeared praying for divine intervention, when in reality he was only searching for a way out of his problems. He was no praying man. "Go out! Leave me!" he yelled to anyone close to him.

I was thinking it would take him a few days to buy the kerosene and the explosives he threatened us with. We could have fun with Julija's fiddle and the boy, I thought. "Think of how warm and comfortable the place will be," I told the others. They believed me. As Sammy headed out on snowshoes, the loggers and girls who stayed behind admitted they'd never had a better time. No one telling them how to behave, they toasted each other's health and fed on the delights in the cupboard. Eating, drinking, me with my boy flute player, we went on without closing our eyes, lest it be the sleep of drunken exhaustion. And I always woke to find him true to me. "Your eyes sparkle, your mouth is soft," he'd say and play me something on the flute, "Jul's Waltz" or something. We piled the grate with logs and laughed and danced in the Minnesota night. We decorated each other with dogwood wreaths and for the first time in days the boy learned new songs on the ebony flute. We of the Blue Bell were never so happy. The snow squalls stopped; the moon peeked through. I added sprigs of thistle to his hair and holly to his lips, and with a roaring fire, we danced in the wind. "Come join us," he cried. "Come everyone to the center!"

Such nights continue only so long with desperate men on the prowl. In the Blue Bell, the hangers-on sensed it. In a week and a half, the place quieted. When the venison gave out, no one poured drinks or stirred the stew over the fire. In twelve days, our laughter ceased. In thirteen, the place was deserted. Maarit stole the ebony flute. Julija pleaded another engagement, and the boy decided on a long and happy life at his sister's in Beaver Bay. In fourteen days, the cold returned. I could feel it grip me about the waist and loins. It wouldn't let go. With no one around, how quiet the woods had grown. Deathly still. I looked in rooms to find unmade beds. Arvid and the women had traveled off in my wagons. They'd left no flute for my enjoyment, no horse for my escape, just a camera. I took pictures of rooms that grew cold. In fifteen days, I was certain of his return. That day, as I least expected the noise of the wind in the pines, I spotted a shadow crouching in the snow among the trees. Was it not Big Sammy's, the shadow of one who'd returned to an empty hotel? I wondered. In sixteen days, only I was left—dim-eyed, frightened, waiting. I, Lillian, a woman of forty, peered through the viewfinder of my box camera at Big Sammy, who was below me in the garden resting on his haunches. I could make out only his shadow in the moonlight.

The temperature snapped downward. I stayed bundled before the fire in the dance hall, hearing waltzes of the past echo from the walls. There I waited for my lover Sammy's glorious entrance. On the seventeenth and eighteenth days, I kept the fire going, but hardly ate or slept. We'd dance a two-step across the sawdust floor when he returned. To calm my last moments, I imagined "Halla Trallen" or "Nikolina" would be echoing from the walls as I came forward to meet his fatal embrace. This was one dance he knew well—the Revenger's... what?... Waltz, the Revenger's Polka. After I went out to him and he did what he had to do to me, then Sammy would have the ice palace all to himself. He could wander its halls seeking an end to the curse of that enduring music, that echo of the flute and fiddle of a month ago. Where did it come from, the echo telling him Lillian was unfaithful? Where was the source of the haunting melody? he'd wonder, until he'd driven himself crazy thinking about it.

The nineteenth and twentieth days I passed before the fire. All this time his shadow fell across the moonlit snow when in the evenings I dared to look out. The weather went far below zero. On such bitter-calm nights, I heard the river ice groan above the snap of burning wood in the fireplace. But on the twenty-seventh day, finally, thankfully, the temperature climbed to freezing. Just like that, it broke. In the sunlight, ice melted and dripped from the eaves.

Leaving the fire untended, I opened the door and walked out. In the sunlit, sparkling garden, where in five months or so I'd plant potatoes and tend beans and lettuce, a beautiful, frozen figure crouched on one knee in the frost. Ice streaked his long red hair. His eyes glistened with cold. His mouth was open as though he'd tried shouting to me at the moment the cold stole his spirit. You could almost hear the shout frozen in air. But what was he saying? A message to me to stop the music, that he needed me after all? He had come this far and couldn't get out his message of love, couldn't stumble the thirty steps to the door of the Blue Bell Hotel. Crouched like that, he looked as though he'd have leapt out to embrace me if he could have just shaken loose of the cold tightening about him. He'd held that pose in ice for the twenty-seven days it had been below freezing. I knew if I found a spot for him under the pines, I could enjoy Big Sammy's threats and stares, enjoy his violent temper, for a good long time yet before the return of spring.

The Pulaski Guards

This snowless December I'm back in Superior living with my parents. Cars pass from the Upper Peninsula with four inches of snow on them. The Duluth hills are snow-covered. The gray weather in the lowlands makes people think something is going to happen soon. We cannot remain snowless all month.

Walter Stasiak, Polish American war veteran, United States Marine Corps, I have returned to my cold, gray hometown. While I was in Vietnam, my girlfriend married Steve Doherty, my friends found new friends, and my parents got set in their ways. At the kitchen table in the evening, Dad practices the accordion. With his arthritis acting up, he'll never get "Helena Polka" right. On the living room couch, Ma snores so hard after supper I miss the punch lines on "Rowan and Martin's Laugh-In." Something else: no one is home at my grandmother's house. When dusk comes, my aunt turns on the lamp in the front room, so *Babusia's* place looks lived in.

During a thirteen-month tour of duty outside of Da Nang, South Vietnam, I dreamt of bringing *Babusia* (Grandmother in Polish) a quart of milk on winter evenings. I dreamt of shoveling her sidewalk. In the tropical heat when roads were thick with dust or during the monsoon season when they turned slick and greasy, I pretended

I was home in winter from the war. In the daydream, I was passing her garage, passing her raspberry bushes, her clothesline poles standing like Russian soldiers outlined against a frozen moon. Without telling her I was there, I would shovel her backporch. But there is no snow to complete the dream, just brown grass, brittle trees, and the steeples of St. Adalbert and St. Francis churches rising stark and bare over the East End neighborhood. My ancestors are buried in the cemetery above the Nemadji River, a cross over their graves. My grandfather—*Babusia's* husband—is there. Superior is the land of graves and crosses. In the floodplain below the cemetery, river ice creaks and booms. In the moonlight, the beams of the railroad trestle make crosses on the river. I know the words for Christ's passion: cross, crucifix, crucifixion. I prayed in Vietnam to know every word I could about Him.

If it weren't for school, I'd be lost in Superior the way I was in Vietnam. The weather and four years in the service have thrown me off, dislocated me. With the G.I. Bill, I have enrolled in auto mechanics at the Vo-Tech. At nine a.m., I sit in my car before classes, staring at the East End business district—six stores, four bars, two churches, two cafés. Except for my girlfriend's marrying and *Babusia's* going to the hospital and now the rest home, nothing has changed. The same people walk into the same businesses, come out with the same goods. After automotive classes, I'll drive to the Polish Club at Winter Street and Broadway near the railyard, where the sign out front reads: "Thaddeus Kosciuszko Fraternal Lodge. Weekly Meat Raffle, Wednesdays." By eight in the evening, I will visit *Babusia*. I have nowhere else to go.

"*Dzień dobry*," Mr. Kuzniewski, the bartender, says when I come in in the afternoon. He wears a white dress shirt and gray dress pants from an old suit. He knows my uncles and my old man. "*Władziu*," he calls me. His hair shines under the lights. He oils it, combs it straight back. He is frail and neat. His glasses look too big for his face. No one is here. When he sees me look around at the empty bar, he says, "You watch. The people will show up." Though Pulaski and

Kosciuszko rooms upstairs are reserved for lodge members and for the women's auxiliary to use at meetings, the downstairs bar, where the meat raffle takes place, is open to the public. If it was only for Kosciuszko Lodge members, the bar wouldn't have many customers, but the sign says PUBLIC WELCOME. Next to the whiskey, brandy, and vodka bottles lining the back bar hang packages of beef sticks and salted fish pieces, pizza menus, a calendar, a neon *Na Zdrowie* sign. A jar of pickled pigs' feet in cloudy water nestles beside the cash register.

"Your Grandma Stasiak's not feeling good I hear," he says.

"It'll make her happy if I join the club. Walter Stasiak, Polish Club Member in Good Standing. How do I get in?"

"Fill out the application form. Bring it to the next meeting. During winter we meet at two on the first Sunday of the month. In January you'll get sworn in. It's all changed these days. Our lodge is not like it was. We're barely hanging on. Everyone's old. The Society of Saints Peter and Paul, the Pulaski Guards—all the Polish and Slovak Fraternals formed into one, the Thaddeus Kosciuszko Lodge, in 1928. Now we got no future. Look at me. I have aches and pains starting already this afternoon. It's the dampness."

Rubbing his knuckles, he takes a glass from the rack. Five minutes pass as he polishes the glass with a towel, walks to the tap, pours the beer, empties an ashtray. I look at the sword *Kapitan* Smigiel of the Pulaski Guards wore during ceremonial functions in the '20s. In parades he rode a white horse and held the drawn sword before him.

My grandmother is older than Mr. Kuzniewski, the club, and *Kapitan* Smigiel himself, I think. The scroll on the wall listing the war veterans from St. Stanislaus' and St. Adalbert's parishes, the sword in the display case, the map of Poland on the wall—none of it is as old as her. Despite her age, her skin is soft, her hair whiter than the snow we do not have. Always she knots her hair in a bun. The ribbon she tied the wreath with couldn't be as deep blue as her eyes. In a procession she'd carried the wreath made of wheat and rye. Others in the harvest procession tied together bunches of apples, plums, and pears. This was in 1895. She was ten in Poland.

Today it's seventy-two years later, December 12. Five months ago, Mother wrote me that Grandmother, at age eighty-two, still could bake, wash dishes, and scrub the kitchen floor. When I got back to the States, then home to Superior, I went to visit her each morning. She poured coffee, put out a plate of pastry. "It's okay," she said. "Famine and wars in the old country. Here you don't worry. Eat, Walter."

"Hunger will lead a fox out of the forest," I said, happy to remember a saying from my youth. She repeated it in Polish, "*Głód wilka z lasu wyprowadzi.*"

Now on this Wednesday afternoon of a meat raffle she can't walk or stand. Probably everyone at St. Adalbert's and in the club has heard how she'd fallen to her knees while my aunt was at the house, fallen while I was there. "Where they take me?" she'd asked after she'd fallen a third time. This was at Mass. It was as if history wouldn't let her go forward. She'd grown quiet in the hospital that Sunday after church thinking that once they'd hovered over her and performed their tests, she'd be free again. To humor her, all week they called her the Polish word for "gentlewoman" instead of Mrs. Stasiak. "Are you awake, *Pani* Stasiak?" the social worker had asked her the last day in the hospital. "We're moving you to a place where everything will be normal for you."

"All I want is go home," *Babusia* had said, upset being driven anywhere when they'd told her she could return home. After an ambulance attendant put a blanket around her, draping a towel from her head down around her ears to form a hood, another one wheeled her out.

"Where they go take me? They break their promise."

"We live in Superior remember, Grandmother. I'll go in the ambulance with you. We're in Duluth."

Saying she was cold, that there were strangers about, soldiers, she fussed with her pearl rosary. Things were changing. I wondered what she was thinking. Was it harvest time, the feast called *Dożynki*?

Are you in the old country, Grandmother? I wanted to ask.

That was a week ago we brought her from St. Luke's. When I saw her last night, she was in a bed staring at a corner of a room in the place my dad, her other sons, and my aunts thought she should go. She'd been causing problems during the hospital stay. Now in the nursing home, she'd been speaking less to them in English. From listening to her all my life, I knew more Polish than my older relatives. All their lives, they'd wanted to get away from Polish, from hearing about the old country. On the phone at the nurse's station, my father was telling my Uncle Bill that *Babusia* had been calling for her mother. "Imagine it, she wants her mother. This place is loud. People are crying all the time. I never thought it would be like this." He was almost in tears.

I wonder whether she'll get home before the snow falls. Though my father tells her, "Don't worry. Your stay in here is temporary," he and my uncles argue about what to do with her. My father wants the house sold to pay the hospital and nursing home bills. "He is rich who owes nothing," he says. But my uncles want Grandmother Stasiak's house rented—or they want their kids living there. My aunts think we should wait to see about Grandmother before doing anything drastic with the house. One aunt has washed her hands of the deal.

Babusia counts on me more than on her daughters and sons, including my father. She asks me to bring her things. She tells me stories about her life. She shouldn't rely on one person so much. After Vietnam, I can't count on myself. All I can do is tell her I'll join the Kosciuszko Lodge of the Polish Club. I'll win the meat raffle, too. "You promises no goot," she says when she doesn't feel well.

Last night I told her again, "I want you to believe me about the raffle." She was sitting in a chair.

"Noisy cow," she'd said. "*Mało mleka daje*...noisy cow give little milk.' You, your father, your uncles say teese nice things to me. All you noisy cows. I want to go back to my bed. I want to sleep. I feel sick." She'd grown smaller, thinner, having less to smile about than the day before or the day before that.

"Can't you believe what we tell you, Ma?" my Uncle Ed had asked.

"You tell me and tell me," she'd said before switching to Polish to shut us out. "*Krowa co dużo ryczy.*" All she wanted was her mother in the old country.

Membership in the club will do me no good, I think. Having nowhere to go with my friends gone, with Cynthia married, if I join just to fulfill a promise, I'll end up once a month with forty old-timers in an upstairs dance hall listening to the minutes of the last meeting, hearing the sick director's report, hearing members gripe when someone wins the attendance prize two months in a row. I've heard from my uncles how it was at the meetings they used to attend. After the closing prayer (if I join the club), I'll have a bottle of beer with my free drink ticket and visit with Mr. Kuzniewski. Meeting after meeting it'll be like this. A real future! Before long I'll be a middle-aged working stiff, a mechanic laboring in the Duluth Transit Authority bus barn, on the railroad, or at the East End Mobil. I'll have less hair, suffer indigestion, complain about a sore back or fallen arches. I will become like Mr. Sitek, Mr. Ostazewski, and Mr. Kosmatka, drinking at the Polish Club to forget who I am. I've promised Grandmother, though. A twenty-two-year-old Marine through with active duty, I will remain faithful to the Corps and to her.

"Can I borrow your pen?" I ask the bartender.

When I fill in the application form—NAME: Walter Stasiak DOB: 10/18/1945 ADDRESS: 2531 East Third—I have to cross out the last part where by accident I've put *Babusia's* address. I write across the top, "Semper Fidelis."

"It's the Marine Corps motto," I tell Mr. Kuzniewski when he pours me another beer. He fills his own glass a quarter full. To pace himself, he does this four times an afternoon. Beer comes free with the job. When my beer arrives, I feel better about failing my courses at the Vo-Tech, about Cynthia, about the future of the Polish Club.

Babusia has told me a story. She's recalled how, in Russian-held Poland (it is 1895, a snowless December in her story), she'd waited for the dark with her mother and father, my great-grandparents. Beneath a cloth on the table, they'd let her spread a layer of straw. My great-uncle Piotr, her brother, was serving in the Russian army. Grandmother had sent him thin wafers, *opłatki*. With something holy from home, he wouldn't be lonely among the Russians. Unfortunately, without him there were three people at the table for supper. On this night, Grandmother has told me, you could not sit with such an odd number. Though hungry for the pike, the potatoes, and the mushroom soup, the family always followed the old customs. The lighted candle in the window offered them hope. In Catholic homes in Poland, it is a belief that God—in the form of a stranger—might see the candle and stop to share the meal if an even-numbered place is set at a table. "A guest in the house is God in the house. *Gość w dom, Bóg w dom,*" she'd said. When she stopped talking, all I heard was the heater tapping its cadence in the room. This and the loud voice of the man in the next room. She'd looked around, tried to reorient herself to America. "My slippers," she said. "Don't forget my slippers."

"I'll bring them tomorrow," I told her when I left.

"Do you know what '*Gość w dom—*' means?" I ask Mr. Kuzniewski.

"A guest in the house," he says. "Are you playing the raffle for fifty cents a ticket?"

"I'm going to win," I tell him.

"Not if I do," says a man who comes in. Tassel cap pushed back on his head, belly sticking out, the newcomer rummages in his parka for beer and raffle money. "Last week I got ten pounds of hamburger and a chuck roast." When Mr. Kuzniewski brings him a beer, he sips it confidently, orders another.

Railroad men, city laborers, the evening bartender drift in next. They stomp their feet, say "*Zimno*. Cold." By six, club members with their wives, the housekeeper from St. Stanislaus Church, and the senior high football coach are here. When the jukebox starts, meat raffle traffic grows heavy. Forty people crowd the bar, sit at tables. All these people, and I am lost.

On the wall opposite the bar hangs the case I look in so often. A portrait of Cardinal Stefan Wyszyński, the Primate of Poland, rests against one side of it. A map of Poland stands on the other side of the case. Above seven books with Polish titles is the sword with the flower-engraved handle. Marine Corps officers carry swords at special functions. In parades *Kapitan* Smigiel carried the display-case sword when he led the Pulaski Guards on his white horse down Tower Avenue. You saw men with swords, too, *Babusia*, I think. Your brother saw them. He saw Russian officers and *kozacki*, cossacks.

"Fifty years ago, the Pulaski Guards of Superior wore uniforms like Casimir Pulaski wore in the American Revolution," Mr. Kuzniewski says. "Who remembers Pulaski or Kosciuszko in America?" He reaches in to withdraw the sword. "Here, hold this a minute. Poland is not lost with you home."

Until he calls me "*Kapitan*" Stasiak, I think he is joking having me hold the sword. He remembers my grandfather, he tells me. He appreciates that I see my grandmother night after night. An old-timer, Mr. Kuzniewski thinks I am an officer in the Marine Corps. When he replaces the sword and hands me a raffle ticket from the roll of paper tickets around his wrist, I say, "I was an enlisted man," but he doesn't care.

"You're a captain here," he says. "I hope you win, *Kapitan*."

From the kitchen the manager of the Kosciuszko Lodge parades out with a cardboard tray bearing the first meat of the night: six stuffed pork chops. The meat decorated with parsley, the tray is wrapped in cellophane. "Here's your chops. Buy your tickets from Kuzniewski. Buy your drinks at the bar," he says.

With G.I. Bill money, I purchase four tickets for *Babusia*. When Mr. Kuzniewski has shuffled to every table in every dark corner, the manager, coughing from the stale air and smoke, draws a ticket from a metal drum on the bar. Mrs. Matuszak whoops when she wins. She wanted the chops more than the chicken breasts. The chief of police and Mr. and Mrs. Wojciechowski win the next items—a half ham and three pounds of thick-slab bacon, respectively. What would *Babusia* do with them anyway? Then I tell myself I will win for her on principle, so that she can see I'm no noisy cow like my father. That I can't be sworn in to the Kosciuszko Lodge until January will disappoint her, but I can win the raffle, I think.

"We got breakfast links, ten maple-flavored, ten plain. Be a hit with the old man before you send him off to the coal dock tomorrow, ladies," says the manager. When he reads the number 2-9-8-4-2, no one claims the prize until Mrs. Zowin, having found her glasses, jumps up so fast I think she will have a heart attack. Devoted to meat raffle Wednesdays, she has taken the bus uptown from the East End. "*Kamouszka,* Godmother," the manager calls her. "Come over and get your breakfast links." She kisses him when she does.

With me representing *Babusia* and the night still young, Poland is not lost, I think. But I am off by ten on the next tray. Seventy-two years ago, *Babusia* waited for a guest to fill the fourth place at the table the way I wait for a winning number. It is like I am in the old country with all the broad faces here, the high cheekbones, a few broken noses among the crowd. I can see my own face in the glass window of the display case.

"Sirloin tips," says the manager. Meat is coming fast and furious. Raising his voice, he balances a tray over his head, stopping at tables to show the meat. Mr. Kuzniewski follows him. This time I come close, but the St. Stan's housekeeper wins for Monsignor Nowacki, who is fat enough without sirloin tips. After the bratwurst tray, another boneless chicken breasts tray, and two more hams, I think I will finally have luck when the manager says, "KA-bobs. We got KA-bobs," emphasizing the first syllable.

As if my life depends on it, I buy twenty tickets for ten dollars. Everything slows. The business manager says, "KA-bobs, KA-bobs." Mr. Kuzniewski passes in slow motion. When the manager reads the numbers, the sound comes as if from underwater: 9 1 0 0 5. I have an 0-5 on one ticket. The rest are nowhere close.

Finishing my beer, I can't bring myself to look at the sword in the display case when an old guy asks, "What's the next raffle item?" and the manager says, "Sorry, that's it for tonight."

Crumbling the losing tickets, I throw them in the ashtray, order another beer. As I wait for the place to clear out, I hear people say what I knew all along—that it is snowing.

"Bad luck. I told you," the man in the parka says to me. I am carrying nothing. He is carrying the kabob tray. We step out into the snow together.

"Good thing those kabobs are wrapped," I say as I brush off my car.

It is hushed and quiet in the nursing home. "Grandma," I whisper when I come in. "Look." I lay the lodge application form on her blanket.

"You promises," she says but softly so I can barely hear. She's half asleep.

"I'm joining up at the January meeting," I tell her.

"In drawer...*Swieca*," she says. When I don't understand, she says it again. "You light for me now."

One of my uncles must have brought them. I light two holy candles. They are for the sick and dying. They illuminate a corner of *Babusia's* room. Halfway up the corner, the candlelight grows into a shadow. All her life, I think she has been located at the place of shadows coming from the old country. How much of her has stayed behind there? I wonder.

"Do you feel better, *Babusia*?" I ask. It is a custom that the candles comfort her, I think. When they are sick or dying, the old people can watch them flicker. The candles must tie them to their homes, make them remember others who were sick long ago—grandmothers, grandfathers, uncles, parents.

So you were hungry for the pike and the mushrooms, yet there were three of you, I think. With a candle in the window, the straw beneath the tablecloth, and the eastern star in the sky, there came the knock at the door. Great-grandfather opened it, expecting your brother to come in speaking the hated Russian as a joke.

"*Pan* Handlovsky!" Great-grandfather had exclaimed. You told me this, *Babusia*. Over and over, you have told me how the man said, "*Przez posły wilk nie tyje...* The wolf doesn't fatten on messengers, I hope."

On that night, with the candle in the window for you to expect the Christ-child or your brother, who now but *Pan* Handlovsky should show up with news of a cow. Whether he was a Ukrainian, a Lithuanian, perhaps a Polish Jew, you never told us. You said he was a trader who had talked about livestock that afternoon with the landowner. He told Great-grandfather, "The cow is yours, Adam!" Great-grandfather had reached out to him, you told me. "*Panie* Jezu Chrystus!" he'd said. He embraced the visitor. You could eat the pike and mushrooms now that the problem of the cow was resolved, *Babusia*. You danced and sang. As *Pan* Handlovsky had vodka, you wondered about the power of the candles. It was true then, the custom: He had come, if not in the form of a stranger, then as someone you never expected, you've told us. You sang some more. He had nowhere to go this night the way I, your grandson, have no one to go to but you. He was not an old man. Still, he was bent over as though the wind had pushed him far away. He'd come across the fields when he'd seen candles in the windows of the houses where he hadn't always been welcomed.

"Some day you leave Poland," he'd said to you, *Babusia*. (You've told me this.)

You were young enough to carry the harvest wreaths then, and you bowed to the guest.

"Anna, Anna," your mother had said. "You going to America."

With the extra mushrooms, she'd made *zupa grzybowa*, which simmered on the fire.

As you prayed, he bowed his head. Then he muttered blessings of his own. He enjoyed the meal, then the gooseberry pudding and more vodka. *Gość w dom, Bóg w dom.* You have told me the story many times, *Babusia.*

"*Laknacemu wszystko smaczne*," Grandmother says now.

"I thought you were asleep, *Kamouszka.* I won the meat raffle. Kabobs."

She turns her head on the pillow when she hears the news. "You put the candles in window for me," she says. It sounds as though it takes all her strength to do this.

When I move the candles from the nightstand in the corner, that part of the room grows dark. From the windowsill, I remove her comb and brush, place the candles there. It is cold with no moon out, I think. The windowsill is cold to my touch.

"The kabobs will be fine in the car," I tell her. When I say it, the candlelight flickers as though she knows I am lying to her, disappointing her. I think I see an old man outside raising his hands as though he can't wait to see my grandmother again.

"You tell me the song," she says.

I can hardly hear her.

"Do you feel better? Have you had supper, *Babusia*?" I ask. "Should I call someone to bring supper?"

"We wait now," she says. She gives me the application form, slips it from her hand onto the blanket. "You tell me tat song now."

"The Maciek one, Grandmother? 'There goes Maciek through town with a cane at his side... And he sings to himself, *Da-na, da-na*!' Is that the one you long for? Can you forgive me?"

"Other song tell me, then we wait for my brother come home from Russia."

"'I worked... I worked for my master yet one more season.' Is that the one? I joined the club, Grandma," I say, then sing very softly,

He gave me a wild horse to ride on
All I have now is an old plow.

When I kiss her forehead, I tell her again about the raffle. "It's snowing out, too, Grandma. Please forgive me."

"*A ja na to, jak na lato*!" she says, repeating the words I have been singing.

The candles flicker as I continue,

And a young calf, now a big cow,
And an odd duck with a quaint bow,
And a wild horse I can ride now,
And a happy young quail, flying-O, flying-O.

I hear her humming to herself.

"Sleep, Grandmother," I tell her. "I joined the club for you."

"We wait for my brother," she says and closes her eyes to forget the lies I have told her.

Shovel Work

Joe Nord's well pump was drawing sand. For two weeks, the water appeared clear—no sand or sediment in the sink or tub after his shave or after his wife Ula's shower. Then before work on Wednesday or after work on Friday when he was tired, she'd say, "The water's discolored, Joe." Sure enough, it was different shades of brown, even black once or twice. This had been going on for a year—Ula breaking the news like she wanted to upset him.

Was it for *only* a year that sediment had worked its way into his pipes and plumbing fixtures? Maybe it was for as many years as they'd been married. When he moved the handle of the kitchen sink, he heard grit scratch stainless steel. When he flushed the toilet, a plume of dark water rose in the bowl; this occurred monthly. From the toilet tank itself, he'd removed enough sediment to fill a gallon plastic container. The stuff oozed between his fingers like swamp muck as he scooped fistfuls from the murky depths. With everything roiled up in the toilet tank, he wondered whether he wasn't doing more harm than good dipping his hands in there. Ula was no help. Tired of sitting around, she'd say, "I'm going running, Joe. Will you look after things?"

Fine for Ula to prance down a county road in shorts and T-shirt, leaving him to worry about the damage at home. Fine for Ula to go out jogging when he returned from work at the refinery. Fine. Everything fine. She was forty-two, eight years younger than him. She had energy to run for hours. Way out on County Road W or on the forlorn Irondale Road, she listened to "Only the Lonely," "Just Ask the Lonely," and "Mr. Lonely"—or was it "Mr. Blue," Joe tried remembering. KSAD radio on her Walkman ("KSAD. Had a good cry lately?" the DJ answered when she requested "Are You Lonesome Tonight?"), Ula went out in terrycloth shorts with the white trim curving up the outside of the thigh, the sports bra, the gray T-shirt. On the other hand, after a day at Murphy Oil, Joe wouldn't hurry if the house caught on fire. Why exert himself when he was in pain over Ula?

"I saw her yesterday," someone would say at work.

"Where?"

"South Superior."

She's running *that* far now? he wondered. It was 2.8 miles from their house on W, five miles on Highway 105 to town. After such a long distance and back, no wonder she was tired when he wanted supper or wanted his workshirt ironed. One night (with Ula bushed like that), he told her how Burt Johnson's wife, during the height of lovemaking, had conked out on her husband. As though this were a thing to speak of in public, Burt, BJ, bragged in the break room that he was pumping Ethel good when he looked down and saw her snoring. Whether she was awake or not, BJ still had an itch for his wife, Joe thought. That was more than he had for Ula, except for maybe once a year on an autumn evening with a cold front pushing through.

"I think I'll close my eyes a little," she said after hearing the Ethel-BJ story. She was in the recliner-rocker.

"Do that. Sleep. I'll sit here watching TV. You can sleep all day tomorrow when I'm at work, too." At least she'd been courteous enough to sit up rather than tilt back while he was talking.

Didn't a man have a right to tell someone about funny things or to tell someone, his wife, how deeply he felt about the Green Bay

Packers or how his feet swelled in the heat? Seeing Ula doze, he decided against a shower, though it'd been a hot, stinking day at the refinery. "Ula? Ula? You're awake, aren't you?"

It was like she'd dropped off the face of the earth. Watching her chest rise and fall, he thought how this could be Ethel during love play. He was displeased about the napping, the suntan. For years Ula had stayed out of the sun. Now she ran in the middle of the afternoon. A white T-shirt, fresh green running shorts, and clean white socks accentuated her tan. Everything was neat and trim about her, and look at him! She knew his every quirk—how he snored worse in summer, how he enjoyed a can of Beanie Weenies for lunch, how he sat on the couch in his underpants after work. "At least put a towel under you," Ula told him, but he preferred to forget what she said. Married life made him complacent.

Five minutes after she'd fallen asleep in the recliner, he returned with a towel around his shoulders, a spot of Barbasol beneath his nostril. "I got a good shave, Ula," he said.

Without looking up, she stared at the commercial playing for the fourth time that hour on Channel Three. It was for Restless Legs Syndrome. That's it! he thought. I'll take her to the doctor, get her Requip for restlessness. Then her legs wouldn't need to run. Who was he kidding? he wondered. He was the one who needed something from a doctor to get him started so he could love Ula the way BJ loved Ethel. In the gathering dusk, having stretched her restless legs when she got up from the recliner, Ula went for an evening run.

The problem well, which she passed on the way, stood 100 feet from the house. Water rose from the aquifer through twenty feet of sand, through probably 220 feet of hardpan (a compact layer impenetrable by roots), then through fifteen or twenty feet of clay. For the final 100 feet, the cold, discolored water flowed horizontally through the line beneath their driveway, under the house, up through the basement floor to the water heater and to water pipes branching to different upstairs rooms. Accurate measurements are important to a water-pump man or to a well driller who, when he's dug a well, must submit his figures on Form 3300-77A, Well Construction Report, to the DNR. Willie, the pump man, then later Milt, the well driller, came onto the scene when Ula was running ten miles, five days a week. She'd finish lunch and think about running from her husband. I'll let my food digest, then leave him for good. I'll run 200 miles, she promised herself day after day, but after ten or eleven miles, she turned around. Before Milt there'd been the pump specialist investigating matters. When Joe drove down the lane one day, he saw Willie, the specialist, hovering over the wellhouse, Ula jogging in place.

Willie lifted the shingled roof from the box-like wellhouse where Joe had placed styrofoam over two or three mouse holes. Bits of styrofoam littered the floor where something had gnawed it, maybe carpenter ants. From a bed of pink insulation fallen from the walls and seeming to grow out of the floor, a pipe rose two feet, then bent in a U-shape downward to join the pump.

"These old McCormicks were good when they worked, but they have a freeze point," Willie said. "Water had to make it over the U-joint. That's why you have a lightbulb on in there all winter, or everything freezes."

Willie could be describing me, Joe thought. Judging from the look on the water-pump man's face, he knew what it was like for a guy to be left out in the cold by a wife like Ula. How can he not notice something's wrong at my house? Joe wondered. I have aching feet, I don't shave, my cap is dirty, I'm overweight. My God, Ula looks good when she wants to.

"Explain every detail to me," she was saying. "This is really interesting."

"When a well is dug, the pipe has to be joined with the right material or electrolysis corrodes the fittings. Sand gets in the line," Willie was saying. "Maybe your pressure tank is shot, Mrs. Nord. Did you ever think of that?"

"Not really," Ula said.

Joe caught the water-pump man staring at Ula's body. He had some kind of infection, he'd been telling Joe.

"Maybe it's your flow restricter. Maybe your check valve. The check valve could be stuck. You'll get sediment then because the water will rise and fall, working it all up. Rust, sand, everything gets worked up when a check valve is stuck."

When Ula went in to write this down, Joe said, "Maybe it's my wife that's worked up."

"That so? Wife problems? A lot of it these days," Willie said, fiddling with his fly.

"I have well troubles even worse."

"Could be the casing or the sand trap at the bottom of the pipe's rusted. You've got caustic water around here."

"What would you do about it?"

"The only thing is to work it out or get divorced."

"I don't mean that."

"In what way are you troubled? Sex? Plenty of men are troubled by it. My zipper's broken on my damned pants," Willie said. "Sex can be a problem, I'll admit that."

A few days later, Willie told him, "It's your pressure tank." Hands callused from working with pipe sections, from running the backhoe, from doing the shovel work these projects require, he stood half-smiling as though he remembered their sex conversation. Having moved the wellhouse out of the way and positioned the backhoe, he'd dug a hole down ten feet. Around the county, he had a reputation for honest work, but when a well goes bad, you aim for the next level, and he, Willie, only replaced pipes, pumps, and pressure tanks. He could promise nothing with certainty to owners of old wells. A new pump might not be enough. They might need another well. They might need Milt Shelldrake.

At noon, Joe heard the backhoe shut down. The rusted pressure tank, dug from the earth where it had worked hard for years, lay in the weeds at the edge of the gravel driveway. With the backhoe scoop, Willie'd brought it up. A tree root pierced it.

"Eighty-two pound tank, Mr. Nord. Looks like a one-man

submarine. That's how much air pressure you had all these years, eighty-two pounds. Looks like a failed marriage," he said. "If you shared the well with other houses, you'd have needed such a large tank. This swamp country was supposed to be developed, the wells shared. Things happened. Only some development got done. A pressure tank like this could have moved water from your well to two, three houses if the land was developed as planned. The Amtrol-X-Trol tank I put in your basement is half as big as this big, old-fashioned, eighty-two pounder."

He was fiddling with his zipper again. He does it everywhere, I bet. It must be subconscious. Here's a man who, except for the zipper problem, knows his limitations, Joe thought, wondering whether Willie was married, divorced, had a girlfriend or two. Joe imagined him with beautiful women. As Willie talked, he smiled, even with nothing to smile about. It was subconscious like his zipper-pulling. The smile must help him meet women. He had the good looks and build to appeal to them, the stone-blue eyes, the thick chest, strong hands. He was confident of his abilities. You could see it in the way he climbed onto the backhoe, Joe thought, in the way he walked around a hole in freshly dug earth.

"I picked up an infection," Willie was saying, smiling. "I'm happily married. It's nothing at all. I'm taking pills for an infection. You ever have trouble with your pecker?"

When Ula came out, he stopped talking about it. "I'll get my lunch. You should have water by five, five-thirty, Mrs. Nord. When I put in the pressure tank, we'll hook up your garden hose to it, open the screen on the basement window, run the hose out of there. We'll work the well hard for twenty-four hours to clean her out of sediment, rust, just everything built up 220 feet below the surface." With the shovel blade, he scraped the heel of his boot. He was more relaxed than earlier when he'd disappeared down a wooden ladder into the earth. Maybe he'd taken a pill and relieved himself down there, Joe thought, relieved his pecker of its infection.

"I have to go to work. I start afternoons at the refinery."

"We'll take care of her for you if you're not home," Willie said.

Take care of who? What kind of infection? Joe wondered. "In case it doesn't work with the well, can you recommend someone?"

"Milt Shelldrake for sure," Willie said, as if the pump man were in league with the well driller. "He's the next in line after I try a few more things. I can probably fix her. Let me do more thinking." He was eating a sandwich. Offering Joe a bite, he said, "When they put in your well, they backfilled with sand, which is good. It's a lot easier to dig in than clay."

Three weeks after Willie stopped fiddling with himself in Ula and Joe's presence, telling them the well was good to go, Ula said, "The water's discolored, Joe. The problem's returned."

He acted as though he didn't hear her. "Let's eat. Don't do anything funny with the potatoes tonight. Canned creamed corn is fine for me. Are you eating?" Everyday she settled for salads.

"Look at the water," she said, annoying him.

"This was a problem we solved. We've got the bill to prove it. I'm tired of it. I never think of anything else. Why are you trying to upset me?"

"I agree. We had a water problem. We got it cleared up." As the potatoes boiled, she checked whether her running shirt was dry on the clothes rack. "But it's not cleared up. Take the white fruit bowl from the cupboard. Run tap water into it. Doesn't it look a little brown against the white bowl?"

"I paid him. Jesus!"

"He couldn't guarantee we wouldn't need a new well, Joe, even after everything he did."

"I don't remember. I don't remember anything but that it looks like somebody's tracked fresh clay into the house. Was Willie here? Did you let him in? There's chunks of fresh clay in the downstairs bathroom. He has an infection. Look at the clay all over down here."

Upstairs, she was admiring herself in the living room mirror, turning her head to see her profile, pulling her hair down over her forehead the way Willie liked it. "Anybody could have tracked in that little bit of mud. I'll get a wet paper towel and clean it," she said absent-mindedly as Joe fumed downstairs.

When he looked for more to complain about, she went for a run.

"A drill rig and water truck are coming tomorrow," he said when she returned. "It'll maybe cost me four grand for a new well."

"When is he coming?" Ula asked.

"It depends on how deep," he said, as though he didn't hear the question. "Eighteen dollars a foot times possibly 220 feet to drill a well. He said you'd be satisfied."

"We'll be satisfied."

"You will, he said you! Maybe I heard him wrong."

Who except Willie could have expected Milt Shelldrake might be needed in August? It's easy to see why everyone was confused earlier—why Joe Nord had worried about sediment; why Willie, battling the mysterious love-sex infection, had considered options to try before recommending Milt; why Ula had been getting in shape: perhaps it was to find a man to share his infection with her. In retrospect, everything was clear—unlike Joe and Ula's well water.

All through the previous month, he had been telling her stories about Burt Johnson's sleepy wife and thinking, "God, Ula looks great," though for awhile she'd had shin splints and a blister. Now it was August, Milt Shelldrake's month.

Still jittery about water in case the well didn't work, she'd had Joe buy bottled water from the market. This she poured into a pan to wash with.

"I'm going to call Willie to complain," Joe said as Ula cleaned up.

Over the telephone, she heard him: "It didn't work. Sediment's back. The check valve, flow restricter, and pipes you put in will be okay in a new well, won't they? I can't pay you to replace all this. What?" Joe said as though he'd lost the connection to Willie for a moment. "What about the infection?"

It didn't surprise her to hear this when everyone except Joe was infected with the infection of waiting out boredom until you were loved. Joe was bored, bitter. Love was over for him. Thankfully, it isn't for me, thought Ula.

"How's your infection?" Willie must have asked him.

"I don't have one. My wife has cured me. Not a hint of an infection around here."

"Why are you telling him?" she asked when he hung up. "Don't talk about personal things. Don't even tell anyone we need a well. People like hearing about misfortune. They laugh at it."

"I hear about you from everyone, yet you won't let me talk. The guys at work tell me you're running from home. They say you request songs and when you do, you sound sad. When the deejay asks your name, you don't tell him Mrs. Nord, but you use your maiden name."

"I am sad," Ula said.

"I called in a request once. When the deejay asked have I had a good cry lately, I didn't know what to say. I asked for Ricky Nelson's 'Lonely Town.' The deejay said, 'This one goes out for Ula from her husband who says he's at the refinery crying.'"

"I heard it on my Walkman. That was you? I didn't catch the name."

"I got over my tears. I dried them before the boss saw. What do I have to cry about anyhow?"

"The well," Ula said. "There's that and everything else."

"It's no fun," Milt said when he came with his drill rig. "I can tell you it's no laughing matter, the infection. It makes you itch." He had KSAD on, perhaps more out of sympathy for Joe than for entertainment. With Milt infected, that meant Willie and him both! Maybe it was something well drillers and pump men picked up, Joe thought, happy that he was immune and not infected.

Standing in a little space on the drill rig where he found room amid the bags of Quickgel, Milt checked his pants zipper before moving a lever. The generator on the truck rumbling low and loud, up rose the boom that held the drill, the boom moving over the spot they'd chosen for the well. Milt stood with a free hand on his hip, then lowered it again. Milt was no Willie the well man, Joe thought when Milt fiddled with himself the way Willie had a month before. Milt was triple the size Willie was.

"Are you taking pills for what you're doing subconsciously with your zipper?" Joe yelled. It was impossible to hear with everything so noisy.

Milt's assistant slid a mud-caked trough from the bed of his pickup. "He doesn't bother with pills. He lets nature run its course. Look at him. No pills can keep the dam from bursting."

From inside the house, Ula saw what the man in the gray shirt and blue jeans was doing with his free hand. The infection must be uncomfortable, she thought. Done rearranging his jeans, Milt moved by instinct around the truck. He climbed up and down, getting things in place, checking things. He wrestled with four-inch well casing; he spelled his assistant; he shoveled off the liquefied mud that rises from a drilling operation. It takes vigor to do this, but you get lonely on a drill rig.

On the first day, Milt made it to 150 feet. At four o'clock, Ula went out to meet them. There was no shade, she thought, and they've been out here all day. With the generator, the wet mud pulsing from the hose, the assistant raking it from the trough, there was so much commotion all she did was watch a minute, wave, then jog down the lane.

On the run to Barnes Road, she thought of Milt up on the rig. She followed Barnes to where it meets C, which she took to Short Cut Road, following that into the Nemadji River valley, then turning around on Highway 35 to meet C again at the junction. Through the popple woods near home, she spotted the top of Milt's beam, heard the clamor. No doubt Willie had told Milt everything about the refinery man's lonely wife, about what he'd done to her and she'd done to him. She anticipated Milt now reaching out for understanding. The assistant was there to look after things if Milt joined her in the house, which he'd probably do, thought Ula, after the big buildup Willie must have given her.

When love comes, it makes people happy. It boosts their energy, although Ula, who could run sixteen miles, and Milt, who worked twelve-hour days, had plenty of energy—too much in fact. Before their lovemaking, they heard the drill in the kitchen, where Milt, wiping his face with a washcloth, had asked about her run:

"Hot," she'd said. "I'm hot." With a towel, she dried her arms and neck when he came over to do this for her. She never imagined a well driller could be so gentle. Lifting the back of her light brown hair, he lay his hand there a moment to cool her. He blew softly on her forehead. With the back of his other hand, he touched her cheek. Her eyes looked tired. He liked that. He liked that her shoulders slumped. She was a couple of years older than him. He liked her for one other reason—the hip-to-waist ratio he'd read about that says women whose hips were in a certain proportion to their waists were attractive to men. Milt and Willie could have encircled Ula's waist with their hands. Milt, Willie, and the assistant well driller could have encircled her hips. The interest in the ratio comes from early historical times when men sought mates for child bearing based on such features.

Some men are leg men. Some are ass men. Some like a good hip-to-waist ratio. An hour and a half later, when Milt, a hip-to-waist man, still didn't know her first name, Ula was saying, "Infect me. Give it to me, Milt, drill it through my hardpan." Hearing the drill pounding away, they'd made love in the living room, bedroom, and hallway, and they had the attic to get to yet. This sounds like crazy talk, but not to a well driller. He could talk this way, too. He could ask to have his hardpan pierced. What does it matter what lovers tell or ask each other? It's a part of the secret of the infection. Wasn't it better for Ula than being with a man who snored and couldn't wait for his Beanie Weenies?

Exhausted by Milt, Ula could barely whisper her own name

when they went up into the attic, but when she kissed his lips up there and everything started again, she said it, screaming the name as though the future had opened up for her, and he went "Oo-la-la" and fell back on the rafters as the drill quit outside.

"Ula." "Milt," they said to each other, as though they'd met in a new way.

Now she was infected with a version of what the men had. It enabled her, for the first time in years (not counting the dalliance with Willie) to think she could love someone, a well driller in the prime of life. "Milt! Milt Shelldrake!" she said over and over as his sweat dripped on the insulation.

Everything you say about love has an opposite, of course. If you were a man like Joe who, at present, wasn't in love, then you'd disagree with the mysterious, magical things said about it. What is the infection? How did it affect Mrs. Nord? It started with longings arising from her despair. That afternoon with Milt and for a long time afterward, her infection consisted of the physical desire called the "love itch." She caught the itch because, after shutting herself off from the "pleasures that the flesh doth surely hold," she needed, in desperation, to find someone. In real, true love, the so-called itchy phase is followed by a second phase: the desire for the communion of hearts. This is when warmth emanates from the soul.

Is it immoral to connect in this way? Say a person lives for twenty years in marriage getting a hug on her seventeenth anniversary, a pizza on her eighteenth, a Culver's Butterburger and french fries on her nineteenth, a new pressure tank on her twentieth. During the remainder of the affectionless hours, there was nothing. Is it immoral to want something before one's time on earth is up?

Joe Nord those days thought he cared only for the well and the pressure tank. He was therefore angry with himself for calling KSAD. Not having cried since that afternoon at work, he wondered whether the infection might have spread. The way he felt about his wife wouldn't allow him to have the infection; however, a mild strain could be bothering him, he thought, though certainly neither the full-blown phase-one itch nor any of the maturing-love stages. Since the itch phase of years before, he'd gone to a phase where a disappointed refinery worker begins to suspect his wife of having an affair. That is why he requested the Ricky Nelson song again after two weeks.

There's a place called Lonely Town.
Where you cry your troubles away.

Joe was in a bad mood when he came from the refinery after the first day of drilling. It was hard telling about him. If he didn't have his Beanie Weenies, he'd start to feel bad, and that would be it. He didn't have the energy to shave or comb his hair. He saw no reason to, not for Ula. Now there was no tap water, and she was saving the bottled water for morning coffee.

"It's a mess," he said. He was talking about the world in general. Through the picture window, he saw the outlines of the equipment of the well driller. "I don't know what's wrong," Joe was saying. "The mess in here is like the mess outside. I ask you about it, and you don't tell me how the house gets dirty. People say you're running more than I know." He sat on the living room couch, head in his hands. The heat, Ula's distances, the well problems were collapsing on him. "Don't go running," he said. "Where would you go at midnight?"

"The well will get done," she said the way she'd said it for two months already.

At one a.m., he tried loving her, but it was useless. He lay in his sweat pants thinking about guys in the crude unit having a laugh over BJ's wife. He thought about the refinery, whose loading docks and cooling towers covered one square mile of town. Not as tall as the main column of the crude unit where Joe worked, but surely noticeable, was the flare stack. Atop of it, a flame burned "off-gasses" that were of no use to the refinery.

He was sleeping when Milt and the assistant came at eight

a.m. Out the window, Ula watched them. Milt looked as though he couldn't wait to start drilling. She was smiling, blowing him kisses, making a heart sign with her hands when Joe came from the bedroom in his sweat pants.

"I know what it is," he said. "I finally realize."

"It's nothing," said Ula.

"I'll do the truth telling. I know what it is. I'm not stupid. You're making signs to him. You're infected."

Taking out her Walkman, finding KSAD, Ula watched the Milt Shelldrake operation. Milt was dipping a yardstick into the well casing while the assistant lowered the drill a few inches at a time. It appeared they were nearing the end. Milt would pull out the yardstick, put it back in. He must have been getting depth measurements.

When she looked around to see what he was doing, Joe was on the phone calling KSAD. "This is a request. Yes, it's Joe. Could you play 'I'm So Lonesome I Could Cry?'" They waited for it together, Joe listening on the kitchen radio. When Ula requested Brenda Lee's "I Want To Be Wanted," Joe requested "Bye Bye Love." When Ula requested "Heartbreak Hotel," Joe requested "One Is the Loneliest Number." When Ula requested "Brown-Eyed Handsome Man," Joe requested "Love Hurts."

When Milt came to the door, it was time for the noon news. "I hit sulfur on the way down. We went 230 feet. We'll pour bentonite chips in the old well to close her off, then clean up and get out of here. Your water will soon run clear, but you might have a sulfur taste. Nothing we can do about it."

"Just so there's no discoloration," Joe said.

From his zipped-up pants, Milt pulled his hand back.

"That's a bad habit you have," Joe said, Ula calling, "Joe, your request is coming on." Who cared about "Mr. Dieingly Sad" by The Critters when standing at the door was the reason for his sadness? Who cared about anything? Joe thought.

"It is a bad habit," Milt said, dropping his hand so Joe couldn't mistake what he was doing with his pecker. He was looking past Joe to Ula. The assistant had joined them. "Did you tell them how much hardpan there was, Milt?" he asked. "That thing aching? What are you doing with your hand?"

"It never quiets," Milt said.

"It's different for normal men. You could drill rock, Milt."

"There has to be help for it," Milt said. "I read in a medical book that I have 'priapism,' except for in modified form because a man with priapism has 'a persistent erection unaccompanied by sexual desire or excitement' and mine is accompanied by those things, Mr. Nord."

He looked as though he'd unzip himself on their doorstep.

"Catch it, then. Fight it. Wrestle with it," Joe said.

"My disease is accompanied by things that don't allow that, such as my enlargement from the infection and the need for the daily release of love. There's no catching or fighting it. It fights you!"

"The daily release of love?" Joe asked.

"The hourly release," said the assistant.

"There's a song coming on in a minute," Ula told Milt. "Listen to it in the drill rig. We'll listen in here. The song's for you, Milt."

The rest of this concerns Joe at the bitter end. The man without an itch was glad to see the drill rig gone when he left for work at two. He could drive down the lane in peace. For the past months, it seemed as though Willie, Milt, and the assistant had been at his place more than he was.

By late August, Ula was running more miles—in September, more miles yet. Once she had the itch, it was always more, more, more with Ula. She began thinking of running competitively. With Joe home mornings and Ula desperate to get out the door, she'd change into her running clothes and be gone before breakfast. Milt would tell her whose well he was drilling. There she appeared—fifteen, twenty miles from home—leaning against the water truck or standing by the sacks of Quickgel thinking of Milt's modified priapism. Beneath the weight of a lengthy marriage, she had discovered the body of a long-distance runner, a smooth, supple body under Milt's loving hands, which he knew where to apply—to her calves and thighs, for instance, which needed to be rubbed with some degree of pressure. If he so much as mentioned hardpan while rubbing her, she was a goner. Two hours later to loosen up, she'd do trunk twists, a few deep knee bends, then on her way home, think of where they'd meet next time. One day she ran fifty miles round trip, another day, seventy miles to him. Milt shook his head in wonderment when Ula told him ultra-marathoners run 100 miles or more at a stretch.

One October afternoon at the bridge that crosses the Nemadji River a mile down the Dedham Road, she came upon his drill rig parked in the shade. Rock, sulfur, hardpan—nothing slows Milt Shelldrake. They lay right on the rig when Ula asked him to go to work. If you take care of my infection, I'll take care of yours, is what she meant. This is not possible. Infections worsen for people in love. Nothing quells or stops infections. Lovers can't get enough of each other. They might as well not eat as give up loving.

"Oo-la-la," Milt said when he hit that hardpan and yelled her name, and this kept Ula looking for him day after day. Sometimes she did what runners call "interval training"—the Swedes call it *fartlek* training—jogging half-mile intervals, running quarter-mile intervals. Sometimes she did hill work depending on where Milt's work took him. Sometimes she went all out doing nine-minute miles. Milt was no runner. Besides, he had to work. He was the one with the drill rig. Let me say their feelings about each other were mutual. Ula didn't give more than he gave, for she wanted to run. She liked running. Milt, on the other hand, needed her; for of what does the well-driller's life consist but the monotony of moving from place to place, doing jobs, filing forms with the DNR, mailing out bills, etc.?

And during this time Willie, the water-pump man, was out in the county looking into other love matters. So, too, was Ted Trifilette, the rural mail carrier, spreading his infection, and Dan Pince, who drives the grader down Irondale Road and other unimproved roads. No one competes with Milt for an infection, though.

In southern Wisconsin where he used to work, he'd gone down 500 feet. Ula didn't care about the lady well-owner's name in that case, for Milt was all hers now. The wells he'd once dug no longer mattered. How far had he drilled, 400,000 feet into the earth, if you put one well on top of the other? Not as far as she had run or as deep as her heart had been hurt. After twenty years with Joe Nord, she'd convinced herself her hardpan was impenetrable. But Milt and the crazy language they shared while loving made her think differently.

"You've released a very stuck check valve," she'd say, kiss him, and start the process.

"My flow restricter was on the fritz before I met you," he'd say.

"How much is a twenty-foot length of pipe today?" she'd ask.

"Do we have enough Quickgel, Ula?"

"You can't restrict my flow restricter," she'd say.

On and on it went as Milt loved Ula.

What about Joe, the husband with sulfur in his well? While this was going on, he never cared to hear another word about wells or sex. Even if you mixed love up into all of this and called it sex-love, love itch, itchy love, root of love, or devotion to love, he didn't want to hear of it. Give him a shovel, and he'd happily bury all love as deep as his eighty-two pound pressure tank had been buried. He was free of the awful infections of love, as free as his water was free of sediment. But when he came home weary from work and Ula was not in the kitchen and he read in the newspaper about the rural Superior woman, Ula Nord, preparing for a 150-mile race next spring, his water had a sulfur smell that made him gag, though thanks to Milt the color was better.

Hello from Ture

Every winter in Two Heart, Wisconsin, someone is caught after dark where he doesn't belong—in among the big firs or out along the frozen muskeg by the river. Around here idle wanderers better be careful. You may have seen Ture's house. A picture of him straddling its peak where snow has yet to reach was sent across the country by the Associated Press. The intention of the photo was to show how bad Two Heart's weather is. Here's Ture in fur parka waving to a cameraman, who must have been on snowshoes in the garden, to get off his land. At first glance, all you see are gentle curls of smoke, behind Ture the weather vane, then the top of the deep, gloomy woods. Staring hard, you may observe below the peak a crude, wooden sign reading: "Hello from Ture, Helen, and _______." The blank part was for Kruger's name. When he died the winter the picture was taken, Ture ripped down his name. Earlier, Ture'd refused to get Kruger to a doctor. After a month of passing blood, Kruger stopped trying to convince Ture of the seriousness of his condition. But enough of this. How Kruger came to live here is my story, for he was no one's relative and only for awhile a lover to Helen, Big Ture's sister.

In those days, men like Kruger regularly came through Two

Heart. On Saturday nights, four saloons—the End-of-the-Line, the Crow, the Red Wing, and Sever and Eddie's out on the highway—were full of loud, boasting men. Walking down the street was risky business if one of the men turned violent. That was when Kruger came here. Where he'd been was a mystery. As far as we could tell, he hadn't been working nearby—not at the lumber firms. No one forgot him once they'd seen Kruger either. It was crazy, as if one day he'd dropped in out of nowhere, as if he'd decided (for it was obvious by his ragged, dusty clothing he'd been traveling) that our town as well as anyplace could solve the problem of his teeth. He came ahead of a late October storm, groaning and clutching his jaw with one hand, with the other swinging a gnarled hickory stick at anything within reach. Out of fear, good people bolted their doors, pulled their shades.

At the Red Wing, he tried numbing his pain. Lifting his glass, he downed his beer and his snowshoe grog in two gulps. It was as if he were bedeviled the way he clutched the bar. Bellering, he rampaged his stick from side to side. After a few hours, he went to the drugstore for aspirin powder. When it wore off, he complained more than before, so that it seemed nothing in the world would comfort him.

Ordinarily, carrying on like that, he wouldn't have lasted five minutes in the Red Wing before someone called him out. He was neither a tall nor muscular man. But at times the patrons here have a genuine sympathy for wounded or suffering men—except Big Ture, who sympathizes with no one. And so Kruger was left alone. No one came near, afraid that whatever disease infected his teeth and made his gums bleed and swell might be contagious. Because of him no one laughed, sang, or called the bartender, who stood agonizing among them, over this man Kruger.

All this time from a booth in the rear, Big Ture eyed the unusual proceedings. Nobody noticed him laughing to himself. That was the way it went, that Ture was left to himself in the Red Wing. Twice he'd been barred admittance, once for chewing a man's ear off in a fight; once for pocketing change that wasn't his off the bar. Then a few weeks later, he'd be allowed back in. Still, he was *never* anyone to fool with.

Now he sat brooding, laughing, and watching the spectacle of the newcomer. Behind the bar Otto poured beer and snowshoe grog. In the corner Mr. J.T. Rowell struck up his music on the concertina. One look from Ture silenced him. When Ture sidled toward the stranger, who, drunk now, slumped over on the stool, the crowd pulled back. First, Ture relieved the stranger of the hickory stick; then, as if he were examining the teeth of a wild animal, reached up with thumb and forefinger to open the man's mouth.

When he steadied the sagging head and raised the upper lip, he observed a row of teeth that were broken, chipped, or outright rotten. No one had seen anything like this. Nor was the stranger old. Something else had caused the teeth to rot—not age or ill health. Under the soot and grime on his face, a face that hadn't been washed in months, it looked like, were bruised lips and eyes that were (despite the snowshoe grog and the pain) beginning only now to lose their youthful flash. Something had gone so wrong here. Fascinated by the sight, Ture lowered the stranger's head and helped him off the stool.

Ture's adventure in the Red Wing caused much consternation in Two Heart. Not that it was an unusual show really, for he'd been courageous at other times. Those, however, were forgotten when he attacked the preacher with his fists or shot holes in Ed Hollister's boots. The stealthy Ture was nothing for Two Heart to be proud of. Mean, violent, unrestrained, he would smash the nearest object and rail against the universe when he saw himself thwarted in an endeavor. Sometimes his furious shouting actually saved his life by keeping neighbors from shooting point blank into pigpens and chicken coops when Ture stood there with tomorrow's supper in his arms.

"Look, it's Ture," they'd say and retreat into the house.

Before the stranger came, Two Heart tried leaving Big Ture alone. For a time, a person was able to drink in the Crow and the Red Wing without keeping an eye out for him. Men went around congratulating one another. “Perhaps we’ve broken Big Ture,” they said. More and more the shades were left up when he passed by. Seeking to forgive him, people would say, “Maybe he’s just more high-spirited than most.”

That was until Ture stole the train. Something got into him, and one night he made Ham Eudin’s logging run to Brule with the locomotive, leaving it idling at the dam crossing where he’d fallen dead drunk in a ditch. After that he was surlier than ever. After what they did to him, he even refused to drink at Sever and Eddie’s on the highway, where the worst men go. Out beyond the town they had taken Big Ture and lashed him with rawhide until his face and body were roped with blood, then they telephoned Helen to come get him, leaving a note pinned to his underwear that said, “I will NOT steal Ham Eudin’s 8:52, as he needs it for work!”

But once he was denounced and the window shades were pulled down again in Two Heart, there was less cause for fear because, miraculously, Ture stopped coming to town. Even after he’d recuperated and there was only a slight scar above his left eye to remind him of what happened, he stayed away. At the Red Wing, Otto swore up and down, “This time we’ve turned him for the good.”

While out in the cabin by the firs, Big Ture was biding his time. He was licking his wounds much as an animal will, only with the added benefit of his sister Helen’s expert nursing and the oil of several antiseptics she’d painted in red swaths across his neck and shoulders. Then the woods shuddered with his curses, and it seemed he would explode with hate.

There is a popular misconception of what hatred does to a man. With Ture it did not do what, according to this myth, it is supposed to do. He didn’t wither under its burden. On the contrary, he grew tall and powerful so that once his back and shoulders healed, once he was able to get around again, he disposed of his chores with a facility he’d never had before. And all the while he avoided the town.

His hatred, directed against Two Heart in general from the mayor down to the church’s venereal sacristan, was wild and unreasoning. If Ture had a difficult job, he'd add to the poison in his mind by avoiding the sensible approach. In that way he sweated and grunted, lugging hay by the armful up a ladder rather than raising it to the loft with the pulley. In the evenings instead of resting from his labors, he'd walk among the thorns by the river. They'd snag his clothes, cut his wrists and hands.

When he'd not been to Two Heart in six months, he had to see those who'd caused his exile. For the occasion, Ture sharpened his knife. Its shiny blade could split a sheet of paper. He'd practiced throwing the knife, so that his precision was uncanny. From twenty feet he could throw accurately. He tucked the knife in his belt and pulled on his heavy shirt. Before leaving, he pummeled a bag of rice he had swinging from the barn rafters. He ripped the bag so wide its contents spilled before him in a steady, white stream. That autumn day he came to town with the storm shining in his eyes and rumbling in his ears, and all along the way he had to keep himself from shrieking. He could feel the cold knife steel press his belly as he ran, but it was other hurt and pain that kept him coming.

The Red Wing's volume of business increases on Saturday afternoons so that there will always be men like J.T. Rowell who don't know of Big Ture. One reason for J.T.'s ignorance was that he's deaf; another, that he'd come to town after Ture had been forgotten, disposed of by the town council. J.T., who advertised himself as "The One-Man Band," did not know enough to stop his foolish playing when Ture slammed open the door.

At his feet, J.T. places a small, cardboard placard that says: "The One-Man Band wishes you all a long, healthy, and happy life. Good luck! And keep Smiling." This placard Ture kicked out of the way. Undaunted, J.T. began again, playing five musical instruments at once, each of which Ture noticed and reserved a great disrespectful laugh for. First, he laughed at the harmonica J.T. had wired around his neck, then he laughed at the beat-up concertina J.T. squeezed with his trembling hands. On one leg this traveling musician keeps time with a tambourine and a cymbal, the tambourine fastened with bits of rope to his knee, the cymbal to the bottom of his shoe. With each tap of the foot comes a metallic sound harsh enough to drive weaker men from the room. With his other leg, J.T. beats time on a bass drum.

Ture examined all of this while J.T. started to play a schottische. When the music grew irritating, Ture raised his boot high enough to hurtle it down like Thor's hammer at J.T.'s foot, so that the cymbal gave a final crash and J.T. fell atop his instruments. Next Ture made his way to the end booth. From there he scanned the crowd. At once they returned to their beer, as if in their collective strength confident enough to overlook such distractions. Still, the men standing close to Big Ture shuffled in the direction of the wooden door through which he'd lately slammed. At last he has come for revenge, they thought. Now see how he does us in.

But Ture was content. He ordered one beer, then another and another without incident. Satisfied that he had drunk his fill of beer, he called for whiskey, easing down a half pint. Otto began fearing for the bottled goods behind the bar. If Ture threw something at the bottles, what could Otto do?

An hour passed as Ture soaked up his whiskey. Along with his expertise with a knife, his patience was something he cultivated during the absence from town. Where before anything would provoke him, now he smiled, for all outward appearances content with the universe. Except for his knees, Ture presented a composed exterior.

But these he could not control. His knees jerked against the tabletop in proportion to his hatred. As the afternoon wore on, they beat louder and louder. Try as he would, he could do nothing about them. Each time he thrust the knees up was louder than the last. The wall shook where the oak top joined it. Now the men began to notice the banging. It was too late. For several hours, Ture'd been simmering, feeding his hatred with whiskey and beer. Finally, he could no longer wait. He grabbed two bottles, ripped their necks off. One last time his knees jerked up, this time so powerfully they pulled the tabletop from the wall. For a moment it balanced on his lap.

It was then—as Ture was rising to do battle—that the peculiar visitor with the hickory stick burst in, crying and holding his jaw for all the world as if he were dying. Dumbstruck, Ture sat down, marveling at how loud the man yelled with pain. For awhile Ture almost forgot his hatred. He stared and stared at the newcomer. Here was a man, thought Big Ture, who understood pain. Here was someone like himself. He was certain of it.

It did not take him long to bundle the newcomer off. As the storm rattled around them, Ture limped under the stranger's weight. In the midst of the lightning, it began to snow. It continued that way until after dark when Helen unhooked the door and slipped quietly around back to the hogpen where she flung the contents of her pail. On her apron she wiped her bloody hands and left the pail in the snow. Later, the house became silent. The light in the attic went out.

So that's how Kruger arrived in Two Heart, a lumber town in far northern Wisconsin. For two days he chewed nothing but rags, swallowing his blood. He lived on chicken broth and water. The weight he lost cast his features into greater relief. He was younger than Ture'd suspected. Once the soot and grime were washed off, it was clear that here, despite his missing teeth, was a look that Ture had seen only once and Helen never. His features were unlike Ture's. Kruger's hair was light as a wheat shock. His lips, still bruised from pain and Ture's prying fingers, were just now regaining the redness that Helen knew if it kept on would in one week's time be as deep as wild strawberries. His eyes were ice blue. That frightened Helen sometimes. Once in Buffalo Ture had seen a boy like that and followed him all over the docks.

For a few weeks Ture and Helen did not press him about where he'd been. It was enough that he rested. One could already see the changes he'd wrought in the household. Ture put aside his all-consuming hatred of Two Heart; Helen kept the place picked up. Sometimes she forgot herself and wore her hair about her shoulders. At certain moments, with her crazy, hawk-like features tempered by the firelight, she looked almost youthful. Together the three of them sat in the shadows, Kruger nursing his gums, Ture sipping corn whiskey, Helen curling her hair about her fingertips. In that way they came to hear the story of Kruger's eluding the authorities of the State of Missouri and, crazed and half-drunk with pain and whiskey, showing up here one day with nothing but aching teeth, a hickory stick, and, as if by way of introduction, the sullen autumn clouds that dumped a foot of snow on Two Heart.

This is what he told them: in Sedalia once he'd come upon a hobo. For sport Kruger had armed himself with pebbles. Climbing a bluff, he began tormenting the hobo. He dropped a pebble into the river nearby, then a pebble onto the land close to the hobo's head. The old man rose, peered around, scratched his nose, and, curling about himself like an animal, fell back to sleep. At which time—plink, plink—Kruger began dropping pebbles into the river or onto the sand near the hobo's head. No amount of splashing could wake him. Dimly aware that someone was baiting him, the hobo had resolved to ignore whoever it was, leaving Kruger on the bluff in the afternoon sun with nothing to amuse him. This time Kruger found something larger to send down the hill. The boulder lay beside a log. Rolling down the bluff, the boulder, because it was so large, almost stalled before regaining momentum for the trip.

Robbing the hobo of a wrinkled dollar bill and a few pennies, Kruger ran off and hid in the Sedalia freight yards. On his way north, something curious happened. It was as if by magic that first his gums began to swell, then his mouth to blacken, as if he were cursed with some pestilence, some grave abscess. Who can explain it? This penance, this visitation, call it what you will, was something that solved a philosophical problem for Kruger, the one thing that had disquieted his thoughts for a few years. Rambling north, he'd made the discovery that the sore and painful mouth was far worse than what he had done to the old hobo. If this is so, then I can do anything to anyone, he thought. The pain is not as bad as I thought pain could be.

When Kruger finished his story, the hearth fire dwindled. Immediately, Ture promised him a set of false teeth. Though Kruger said it was out of the question, Ture wouldn't hear otherwise. "You'll need your strength," he said. He coaxed Kruger into the shed where he'd kept moist a handful of clay waiting for the swelling of Kruger's gums to subside. He'd shaped the red clay into two horseshoes approximately the size of Kruger's upper and lower gums. He made Kruger bite firmly into one horseshoe, then the other to make a mold for teeth. This done, he melted pieces of plastic over a flame. With so little regard for the town, Ture had come to rely on his own ingenuity. He set himself to making false teeth. He allowed the plastic to cool and set in the horseshoe molds of Kruger's mouth. In less than a week he would have the teeth themselves from the dentist who passed through once a month. They'd make the difference, said Ture.

Try as Ture did, however, Kruger's new teeth did not fit. Hour upon hour, Ture worked with them, filing here and there, but when he put them back in Kruger's mouth, they were always the same. The upper teeth protruded, making Kruger look as if he were laughing. Although they felt okay, they looked funny, none of which bothered Kruger, who saw it as a fulfillment of a theory he'd divined in the boxcar—that he must suffer a little for the pleasures he had in life. I look the same as ever, don't I? he thought as he clicked his new teeth together before the mirror. Ture did not think so.

Nevertheless, Ture was happy. He saw Kruger in an almost mystical light. As far as Ture was concerned, Kruger could do no wrong. In fact, Big Ture started formulating ways to see if his visitor was truly holy, for the more Ture dwelt on Kruger's mysterious arrival, the more he was convinced he was no mere straggler come to the north, no runaway from the Sedalia authorities. What was amazing was the way the newcomer had with magic, the way he could make nickels disappear when right there only seconds before Ture had seen them between his visitor's fingers. It was baffling. Here, Ture thought, is a very wise man sent to rectify the pain I have felt in Two Heart.

And so the two of them, Ture and the wizard-like Kruger with the face that made it look like he was laughing because of the ill-fitting teeth, spent evenings prowling Two Heart's alleys, sometimes probing windows to see if they'd give. Strolling back along the road, Ture would tell Kruger how the town had brutalized him. He told him of the night he'd been whipped bloody for Helen to find; how Helen had pulled him home delirious in her vegetable wagon. That night, because she was all he had, Ture'd spoken to Helen of things he should not have, of things that were better left unsaid between brother and sister. When the newcomer heard how Ture had been treated, he promised the time was not long off when he should have his revenge. This satisfied Ture that his visitor was genuine. From then on, with clenched fists and angry hearts, they awaited Armageddon.

In those days, with the two of them throwing themselves around the place in high spirits, Ture and Helen's home was never quiet. Helen found her solace in apples, paring a winter's barrel in less than a week. And all along Ture and Kruger continued to go to town, careful each night to hide their tracks in retreat along the road. At times so eager was Kruger that he startled Ture, who at least had a reason for what he was planning in town. But what reason had Kruger? Whatever the case, Ture encouraged Kruger's violent dreams. Ture never imagined he'd end up with such a wonderful partner. All through December they were together—in the shed, the barn, the attic. Intermittently during the day, Helen would look up from her sewing to see them adjusting the bicycle wheel or shoveling their way from house to road. Once, she'd surprised them in the root cellar where Kruger was doing something magical with five nickels he'd stolen from Helen's purse.

That month the snow was upsetting to her. She could count on two or three inches of daily snowfall as much as she could count on seeing Ture and Kruger heading to the barn. Each night as she made supper, she watched the snow drift higher up the side of the house, so that she thought if they didn't do something pretty soon she would go mad. Funny how this year she could not face up to working by candlelight at midday. That was what was going to happen, too: if they did not do something about the way they acted and the deep snow outside the window, she would go crazy.

One blustery afternoon not long after she'd begun having trouble sleeping at night, Ture and Kruger left her and set off through the drifts in the direction of the river. Ture had the shotgun propped over his shoulder while behind him Kruger trudged with a sled, an old milkbox strapped to the top of it. That was the day the snow covered the windows, when Ture and Kruger returned arm in arm through the storm drunk. With the milkbox full of squirrels, they'd returned from the hunting trip.

"Where have you been?" she asked.

"See what we have in the box," said Ture. He motioned as if she were not even there. He stood silently, formulating his plans. In this box of squirrels, he had brought his sister something of value from the forest, a miniature cradle carved out of pine. She found it wrapped in waxed paper under the first layers of bloody fur.

By then it was early evening.

At that time of year, it is hard if you are old and should be caught out late, as is evidenced by the couple who froze to death on their way home from the parlors of the Church of Two Heart. But as the days passed before this night when at the stroke of twelve Ture took his revenge, both he and Kruger had become used to the cold. Each degree the temperature dropped brought a ruddier glow to their faces. Whenever Big Ture heard ice snapping in the river, his pace quickened with anticipation, and Kruger appeared to be smiling within the outline of fur that surrounded his face. They were going to town this very night and be done with it.

After a brisk hike among the trees, they spotted the town, stiff and brittle in the night. Ture's heart raced. Where Big Ture raised the clawhammer the first time, frost had spread its delicate patterns over the window. In a moment the window of the Two Heart Cheese

Shop shattered, its pieces flying across the floor, some as far back as the cooler where special wedges of Swiss and Colby are kept. Swinging the clawhammer, Ture smashed the window of the Red Wing next, as if here were concentrated all the sorrow and disorder in his life. Building to building he ran, kicking out windows, sliding the clawhammer across everything that broke, so that in those few moments, reeling with the rare and heady atmosphere of the just, Ture found his happiness. He eyed Kruger, Big Kruger, setting a fire. He longed to be with him in the circle of flame. The fire leapt from building to building, from the Red Wing to the Cheese Shop to the café and all down the street.

Pumping his hands up and down, Ture roared to the heavens. He patted his partner, slapped his shoulders as he, Ture, grinned at the quarter-moon above. On the brisk night air, Ture and Kruger could smell woodsmoke, hear the river's restless snapping. Kruger cupped his hands together. He made filthy gestures. It was as much as to say: if the town is a woman, this is what we've done to her. And Ture clapped with joy. He laughed so hard his belly ached as they stumbled back along the road leading home.

In no time, they were safe, their heavy boots steaming before the fireplace. While Kruger entertained his host, Helen mixed them whiskey and lemon drinks. They laughed so hard tears streamed down Ture's face. This time with his hands and the shifting firelight, Kruger cast shadows upon the wall—a crude portrayal of the love act. Ture had never seen this side of Kruger's talents. He enjoyed it thoroughly. When Helen left the room, he asked for more. So curious was Ture that he followed Kruger's fingers with his own in an effort to find the secrets of his art.

Shortly afterward, worn with the excitement of the raid, Ture gave in and fell asleep at the table, his hands around a bottle. Then something unfortunate occurred in this house by the firs. No shots rang out, no posse banged the door, but in its own way what happened disturbed the forest calm just as surely. It came about as Kruger appeared to be napping contentedly by the fire and after Helen had said her good nights. It was then Ture felt it strangling upward. Through bleary, half-closed eyes, he saw the fire no longer silhouetting Kruger; Kruger's chair was empty. With a gasp, Ture rose. Pulling the air deep into his lungs again, he emitted a savage cry. That somehow Kruger had gone away leaving him forever was what Ture had thought. He beat his hands against his mouth, pounded his fist into his palm—all before he thought to see which way Kruger's tracks led from the house. He threw open the door. Awaiting him were firs and the snowed-in path—but no tracks. So he hasn't left, thought Ture.

When it dawned on him where Kruger was, Ture could do nothing but rock by the fireplace. How long had it been going on? he wondered. A hundred plans crossed his mind. As the sun rose, he had all he could do to keep from shooting her. He oiled his shotgun, sat rocking longer by the fireplace. Finally, he got up to prepare his own oatmeal so Helen wouldn't have to do it.

In the morning Helen and Kruger came to breakfast as if nothing had happened. While she readied the coffee, Ture eyed Kruger across the table. Ture did not let on that he'd seen his shameless sister in the love act. On the other hand, Kruger, the wizard, was like a man come upon good fortune. He guzzled his breakfast, while Big Ture sat staring over the top of his steaming coffee cup. Kruger asked, "Don't you like your eggs, Big Ture? Isn't Helen's cooking just fine?" Kruger asked Ture whether he wouldn't like to scout around town and pick up the news. And all the time, Ture wished that it had never happened, for before Kruger had been so perfect to him. His face had healed now from when he'd come in October, and his hair was as light as ever. Ture's heart was broken. "No, I have work to do here," he said. "You go." He belched. "Take the bicycle why don't you?"

As soon as he left, Ture aimed the shotgun at Helen. She sat in the corner where Ture had flung her. She was sobbing, head between her legs, but he called to her in a soothing, brotherly voice, "Helen, dear." He trained the twin barrels at her eyes. That was when the idea of the burning came to him.

"Please, Ture, let me go to the bathroom. I'm going to be sick,"

Helen pleaded.

"Go right there on the floor. I am going to burn down the place anyway," Ture replied.

Brother and sister sat in the kitchen. Twice, Big Ture walked over and made her place the shotgun barrels in her mouth. He said she was defiled. Then they heard Kruger stomping his boots out on the porch. Ture held back the curtains, smiled, waved for him to come in. Ture hid behind the door when Kruger wiggled the handle and called out, "Well, I'm glad to see you're feeling better, Big Ture." That was when Ture whacked the back of Kruger's head with the butt of the shotgun. Kruger's false teeth flew clear across the kitchen, landing in the frying pan. Stunned, Kruger went to his knees. He shook his head, gripped the table, then rose slowly up. Ture aimed for the broken buttons of Kruger's coat. When the butt of the gun hit his chest, Kruger sounded as though he were exploding. Ture hit him again. This time Kruger collapsed without Ture's having wasted a single shell.

With Helen sobbing in the corner, Ture had all he could do to keep his head clear. He warned her once. When she continued, more hysterical than before, he bent back her arms, which quieted her for a moment. He didn't burn down the house. Instead, he dragged Kruger's limp body into the living room, propping him half on the couch. The false teeth he left in the frying pan.

The next few days, in spite of her aching arms, Helen did the best she could nursing Kruger. In view of their limited medical supplies, this consisted of applying an ice pack to the base of the skull, where purple swelling had appeared as a result of the blow from Ture's shotgun. To Helen it was clear Kruger had suffered internal injury, for although he was awake, even muttering a few words when he was certain Ture had gone out, he was unable to get up, nor could he stop himself from coughing up a sticky mass of blood every few hours. Helen could not stand to look at it. When he was expecting a coughing jag, Kruger would signal her so she could run into the kitchen.

Through this trying period, Big Ture kept mostly to himself, as he was wont to do before he'd met this stranger. He stalked the forest, roamed his land. One morning, unusually receptive to the cold, he marched to the river, cleaned a space, and donned ice skates for a whirl downstream. And all this time, Kruger was dying inchmeal. When Big Ture came by eating a cookie on his way upstairs to the attic, Kruger began asking him if he wouldn't, please, get him to a doctor. It was all he could do to mumble these words and, like magic, blood appeared at the corners of his mouth. Ture did not hear a word, though, and day by day Kruger sank lower. After a month, his face was turned into parchment and bone. This may be another of his tricks, thought Ture when finally, and for the last time, Kruger implored him to seek a doctor. "Bring back a doctor, please, Ture," he said. And Ture said no. "Then at least give my teeth back," Kruger pleaded. But they remained where they were since the morning Ture surprised Kruger from behind the kitchen door.

What is so unusual about the whole affair is not whether Ture heeded his partner and gave Kruger his teeth, but instead how Helen changed in the days following the assault and how she came to make Brunswick stew, for that was Ture's favorite. It was she who astonished Ture. In the end, Kruger lost his will to live. A day or two this side or that could not have made much difference.

When Helen saw Kruger's condition worsening and that any day he might die, she began thinking of herself and where she stood with Big Ture. Her brother refused to talk to her. He wandered in and out and sat down to the table, but talk he would not, which worried Helen. She wondered what he would do to her once the visitor was gone. Although she thought Big Ture would let her stay on, she could never be sure, just as she had learned never to trust the behavior of wild forest things, dead squirrels in the milkbox. And so she made up her mind, and because Ture was stronger, she decided to ignore Kruger, who was beyond help anyway. All day he lay sniveling on the couch, coughing into his hands, and after awhile she forgot to change the nightshirt which became encrusted with blood.

Her new station was the kitchen. The cooking smells emanating from that room, with its huge oven, were enough to bring Big Ture indoors hours before supper even on the warmest winter days when temperatures reached zero and only three inches of snow were predicted before nightfall. The smells were tantalizing, and when Helen baked one of his favorites, Ture stood sheepishly in the doorway. Once it was Northern pike; once it was Applehead pie. Ture liked his pie steaming hot—on top of it a slice of cheese or a scoop of ice cream, which he himself churned in the barn. The first day he had the pie he hollered to Kruger, "Wouldn't a piece go swell right now?" But it had been at least several days since Helen attended Kruger. He hardly had the strength to raise his voice to ask Ture to please get him to the doctor quick.

Then he fell silent, and when Big Ture wandered by eating some delicacy or another Helen had painstakingly prepared—though not the Brunswick stew to which she was building gradually—Kruger stared up questioningly from the hollow of the couch, skin burning with fever. In the days since he'd fallen prey to the butt of Ture's shotgun, Kruger's face wrinkled horribly. It was especially like this about the mouth where, in spite of the missing teeth which Ture in a moment of beneficence had returned to him, the skin was taut, rough, and gullied with ugly seams. The teeth, the buckteeth, served only to heighten the comedy of Kruger's face.

But Helen had no time for him now. Kruger's life would have to run its course, she thought, for she was busy in the kitchen making a stew for her brother the likes of which he'd never forget. That Kruger should die on the afternoon of the stew, that his eyes should roll up and a ghastly breath escape his lungs as brother and sister sat down to their first amicable meal in weeks, was only coincidence.

There were five pounds of chicken in the stew. That is how Ture liked it. There were heaps of lima beans, four ripe tomatoes, and a handful of salt. Coming in for the first time that afternoon, Ture smiled, sniffed the air, and clapped his hands. "What are we having?" he inquired.

"Something good, one of your favorites," Helen said.

Taking her by the hand, he guided her into the next room where Kruger lay straining to look up with dull and glassy eyes at them both. Ture told him how Helen had made a Brunswick stew, how life was not so bad after all. "Can't you just smell the tasty stew?" Ture asked him, but Kruger said nothing, for he wasn't hungry now.

The Sons of the Desert

Oliver Harding, Stan Laurence's business partner, regrets joining the Laurel and Hardy fan club that meets once a month at the Moose Club. He regrets buying a fez like the ones the boys wear when, after lying to their wives about their destination, they head off for a wild time at a convention. The last thing Mr. Harding wants is the vest with SONS OF THE DESERT—LAUREL AND HARDY FAN CLUB—SUPERIOR, WISCONSIN sewn in sequins on the back.

Turning in bed, Oliver reaches for his wife, who wipes the sweat from his face with the sleeve of her nightgown. "It's easy for you to go on long trips. You drive away, leave me wondering if I'll hear from you. It's like I'm paralyzed. I can't move when you don't call me from North Platte or Yankton," she says.

Remembering how his namesake looks sheepishly out of the corner of his eye and touches his fingertips together as demurely as he can for one so fat, Oliver tries the move on his wife. Unable to resist, Cha Cha says, "Oh, come here, ya big galoot."

The tassel on his fez swishes her cheek as he looks down at her during lovemaking. The way she bites her lower lip and squints he knows she's thinking of someone else.

"I'll be home soon," he says when he's done.

"You going out already? You've just come off the road. We've just made love."

"It's still a workday," he says, washing his face and hands.

He wets his brown hair with a comb, combs the moustache. Making a circle before the mirror with his index finger, he dots the center of it the way Mr. Hardy does when pleased with himself.

Outside, the heat is not as bad as inside. Kicking up dust in the driveway, he climbs into the diesel cab. On each dark blue door with its chrome handle, he has Stan's and his names painted, "Stan & Ollie Trucking, Poplar, Wisconsin," then two bowler hats tipped so the brims touch. He listens to the engine.

On the porch, Cha Cha gazes at the bright sky. "Burn it out of her good," he whispers to the sun. During the last month, he's put as much country between them as possible. But who ends up being hurt when he goes? he wonders. Leaving her by herself serves as an invitation to every Laurel and Hardy and Three Stooges fan in Maple, Poplar, and Hawthorne to see what's so funny out at Ollie Harding's place. He might as well put up a sign: I'M GONE. COME SEE HER SUNBATHE. ASK HER FOR A FEEL WHILE YOU'RE AT IT. He wonders whether she wears the fez when he's traveling and she's running around naked in the sun.

Who in his right mind would leave such a pretty thing alone while he hauled a load over to South Dakota, Nebraska, and Iowa? Stan Laurence sure doesn't leave, Oliver thinks. Stan wants to stay here visiting Mrs. Harding. The last trip out, as Cha Cha sunned herself, he, Oliver, suspecting what was going on, cursed and sweated from Spearfish to Sioux City. He'd telephoned home. No answer. He'd sent a post card. "SICK OF HIGHWAY. SICK OF SOUTH DAKOTA." Then he'd phoned again and again and gotten busy signals as though she'd taken the phone off the hook.

Shifting gears, he brings the big rig to a halt, jumps down into the parking lot at the Hacienda, where he knows the other half of the comedy duo will be drinking.

Stanley isn't happy to see him. He's got the sour look drunks get. Having practiced the fluffed-up hair, the English accent for the boys in the bar, he mimics the real Stan Laurel. "Hello, Oliver. You were gone for a long trip."

"I broke down out of Sioux Falls. When you going to take a run yourself? Ain't we partners?"

"I'm thinking about it," Stan says. "I like it at home. When you're gone, I get to hear the phone ring over to your place. Is that you calling her? Cha Cha's never home, eh? No answer? I haven't seen her lately."

"What do you mean she's never home? She's waiting for me at this minute. I'm not hurrying. That's right. I'll stay here." Enjoying the bar fan's steady sigh, he orders another beer. The breaths of stale fan air are better than the heat and sun outside.

"So who says she out home?" Stan asks his comedy partner. He has a way of getting under Ollie's skin. He has lots of reasons for doing this—old grudges, jealousy. He scratches his head, smiles, mouth curving up in the v-shaped smile. "I'm just trying to help you, Ollie," he says.

Stan's question about Cha Cha troubles him. Suppose she is skipping out on me, he thinks. But hasn't she promised me something meant for man and woman later on? "What business is it of yours, Stanley?" Ollie asks the thin, drunk Mr. Laurence.

The Hacienda has a catfish platter and karaoke on Fridays. The men in here are hard workers, too—farmers, millhands, truckers, even a hard-working comedian, he thinks. There's a lot to like at the Hacienda. Calming down, he does his Oliver Hardy routine. He does it again out of spite. Things get to him—the heat, the taunting Mr. Laurence, the lying sunbather. Mr. Harding imitates Mr. Hardy of the movies in order to make himself feel bad about his wife. He has the bowler hat on he's brought from the truck. Stan's wearing his. They keep it for him behind the bar. With the hat on, Ollie asks, "Why don't you do something to help me, Stanley?" Where the comedian would flutter his tie, Oliver uses the front of his shirt. "I'll be right back," he says.

Buying Stan a beer, he goes to check something in the truck, then starts walking. I'll leave the rig for him. It ain't so far that I need a ride, but I can have one with one of the guys if they come by. I know them and can get a lift, he thinks. Otherwise, I can hoof it.

He does the Oliver Hardy routine in the middle of the road. Dreaming of Cha Cha, he lifts the bowler, flutters the shirt front, whistles the theme that ends with a cuckoo clock going off. Weeds grow through the pavement. Across the fields, dust rises from the parched land. It is the second hottest, driest summer in northern Wisconsin. She's lucky having the creek, even though it dries up most summers. He thinks of her letting the sun tan her brown. She's beautiful. Will the creek go dry again? Will she sunbathe beside it as it trickles its last? Will his neighbor and partner Stan be beside her as he, good ol' Ollie, the fat one, the lonely one with stubby fingers, guides the eighteen-wheeler to places unknown? The crazy cuckoo goes off in his head.

Out of nowhere Swenson's bull lopes over the brittle pasture in such easy strides that Oliver doesn't know when he himself begins to speed up his pace, as he's seen Stan and Ollie do in "Sons of the Desert." It is as if he's trying to out hurry the bull, the creature keeping up with him, halting when he halts, charging again, a huge thing on the other side of the fence shaking its head as if—hearing the rumors about Cha Cha and Stanley—it can't get them out of its ears. Now Oliver is running, mind filling with Cha Cha thoughts. As the bull plods on, its leathery bulk distresses the comedian. Ha-ha-ha, Stan would be thinking if he saw this. As the bull passes him, it seems to Oliver it outwits him as well. Trying to keep abreast of it, he falls behind. Cicadas screech around him. The shriek grows loud. He clamps his fists to his ears—the rumors. It is difficult to concentrate until the bull veers off in search of someone else. "I'm coming, Cha Cha, honey!" Ollie says.

He thinks of Stan and his smirk. He thinks of the fine mess Stanley has gotten them into this time.

In the valley below are the house, the white bridge, the creek.

No one's down there, he thinks. His breath comes hard. "If she's in the kitchen, I'll be happy." He wipes his flushed, angry face. Why doesn't she answer? he wonders.

It is no cooler in the living room. Confused, he runs through the hallway. God, his head pounds! It feels as though something's in there behind my eyes, he thinks. Once before it'd hurt like that when Cha Cha hurried past him as if getting back to the house before him could have saved her. It was crazy. When she got home, she denied being outside. With his own eyes, he'd seen her in the early August darkness. He'd stopped her on the hill. Right to his face a minute later, she had denied it. She even denied he'd spoken her name and looked into her eyes as she, his wife, Cha Cha Harding, slapped his face. "Fool!" she'd said. She'd spit out the word and right to his face later denied saying it, slapping him, or going out at all. She denied it when every star above had looked down to witness it.

"This time I won't believe her," he mutters. "I won't wait for her to come home."

No, this time, he thinks, bursting out of the empty house, running with renewed, violent effort in the direction of his neighbor and partner's farmhouse on the hill, this time, no longer loyal to the Sons of the Desert, Mr. Harding thinks how he, a renowned comedian in a bowler hat, will interfere with Mr. Laurence, who is already interfering with Mrs. Harding.

The Wood-Bat League

I am Matt Folner, left fielder, Green Bay Bullfrogs. On May 30, the day before yesterday, we opened the season at Joannes Stadium, Kurtz Avenue, Green Bay. Tonight on the chartered bus, our second home, we are traveling the farthest north I've ever been. This is the life in the wood-bat league—a game every day for a little over two months, living with a host family, long bus trips.

I play college ball at William Penn, Oskaloosa, Iowa. A history and physical education major, I hit .420 my freshman season. In college we use aluminum bats. Coach Al Perry said I could improve my swing playing seventy-four games in a summer collegiate league where bats are wood. He knows Boyd Barton, my Green Bay coach. "You will have a great summer on the playing field," Coach Perry stated to me in Oskaloosa, "and you will see cities like Madison, La Crosse, and Eau Claire, Wisconsin, and Rochester and Duluth, Minnesota. Are you man enough for it, Matty?"

"Coach Perry, I am the strongest man in the world," I told him.

After downing the Wausau, Wisconsin, Woodchucks in a two-game, season-opening home stint, 1,500 in attendance both games, we are on the road. It is 11:50 p.m. The highway is pitch black on the first night of June (my nineteenth birthday and when I am hitting

.333 with seven at bats).

After games in Duluth on Lake Superior's shore, then in Mankato against the MoonDogs, we will return in glory to Green Bay, Wisconsin, where I stay in the Zybrickis' finished basement on Walnut Street. They get free game tickets for hosting me through the season. It is comfortable there with cable TV, a big futon, my own bathroom. They are nice—Connie, Tom, and their daughter, Wendy Zybricki. I feel lost sometimes with them, though. I have been away from home nine days and wonder what I am missing in Oskaloosa.

On the road, we stay in motels. My road-roomie from the University of Hawaii—a second-year Bullfrog out of Portland, Oregon—is a Green Bay favorite who hit .215 and led the league in stolen bases last year. In a league where the ball doesn't jump off the bat the way it will off of an aluminum bat, .215 is a good batting average for a shortstop. Plus first you have to adjust to hitting with a wood bat, which sometimes takes half the season.

When he puts out the reading light, I ask Jason Spagnolli why he didn't play for the Euless LoneStars of the Texas Collegiate League.

"I could have, but it's too hot to play your best when every night it's a hundred degrees at game time."

"How is it where we're going?"

"Last July we had two games there. It's an old ballpark by some kind of ore dock."

To me it is marvelous, this traveling and living away. I have not traveled like him. To Jason one plane trip to the mainland during the college baseball season to play at San Diego State or Wyoming is farther than we'll travel all summer to places like St. Cloud, Brainerd, and Alexandria, Minnesota, home of the Alexandria Beetles baseball club.

"Do you have a girlfriend?" I ask him.

"I sort of do," he says, pushing his seat back to rest.

"I do," I say. "She did not want me coming here. Coach Perry was a different story. Leaving would be to my advantage, he said. It would be good for me to get away from Becky."

I want to show the league-leading base stealer of last year's Northwoods League her picture, but I have a tendency to talk too much. "This summer she's working on campus. Her dad owns an insurance business. I had her in classes. You see how tall I am? She goes up to my eyebrows, I bet. She is thin. I like girls like that."

"Shut up for a second," he says. He is not really angry. As we pass through the gloomy woods, it is best to keep quiet about Becky. I have been given a chance by her. Not that she said, "This is it between us. It's over." No, she cooled it around me as though she would never trust me after what she learned last month. I should not trust her, yet if this is what it takes to have her as my girlfriend—if it means a second chance for me that we're still talking and text messaging—then I must make good on the opportunity she is presenting me.

"Jason, I am going to look at your magazine," I say. I think he has nothing playing on his headset and wears it to keep from hearing me. On the floor of the bus, *Total Texas Baseball* magazine, which the Euless LoneStars coach mailed him, is open to the pages describing the league he could have played in. You can read rundowns of the teams—the Plano Blue Sox, the Coppell Copperheads, the Denton Outlaws, the Graham Roughnecks, Euless, etc. There are stories on the other wood-bat leagues Texans are playing in, such as the Alaska Baseball League, the Coastal Plains League, and the New England Collegiate Baseball League. The best is the Cape Cod League.

In *Total Texas Baseball*, I see no mention of our league. We sure are in the north woods. Off on the side of this road, Highway 29, we have passed the Up North Bar and the Bear Trap Café in the past three minutes. Their neon signs look lonely at this hour. We have gone through woods taller than any in my home state. In the headlights I see the edge of them and the top of them against the sky. In the window I see my face reflected as though, out there in the dark, another side of Matt Folner is following the side of Matt Folner riding inside of the bus. "Matt Folner, what are you doing in Wisconsin?" I ask myself. The reflection looks sad, though we are the same person. I stare at it. I stare for a long time at the outside blackness, the black window, the forlorn face with blue, sad eyes and light brown hair I forgot to comb after the shower in Green Bay. I miss more than my girlfriend. I miss my parents, my dog, my bed.

Arms crossed, Jason has his headset on to shield him from my conversational skills. His baseball cap tilts forward to shade his eyes. Our logo is a bullfrog with large, white eyes. He is swinging a wood bat. He has a red tongue that curls to the side like he is anxious for the next housefly or the next pitch. Mostly, you notice the green and the whipping tongue. It is neat, but with Jason signaling me by pulling his cap visor lower, it is no use telling him about Becky Osterholm. He is worn out after the flight from Hawaii to the Midwest—followed by two night games and a six-hour bus trip. I am worn out when we reach the Super 8.

There is no call on my cell phone from the Zybrickis, my folks, or Becky. I go to bed thinking of her. I dwell on her speaking to me of marriage, saying, "What if this happens or what if that happens, Matt?" She asked me the question about marriage so often I finally said yes to her before leaving for Green Bay and stared at the wall or at my reflection in the window of her house. I am troubled, but I sleep until nine when Jason turns on Regis and Kelly with the remote.

"Can't you shut up *ever*?" he asks. "I heard you talking."

"In my sleep? Did I mutter a girl's name?"

"Who knows? It sounded like a bad dream."

When Regis welcomes his first guest, I step onto the motel balcony.

"How is your weather?" I ask Becky. Over the cell phone I hear the TV stars in the background in Iowa, too.

"The weather is okay."

"How's everything? Do you miss me? What are you doing? How are you feeling about things?"

"Okay," she says. "I'm okay. Happy Birthday."

"That was yesterday. Is it all you can say? What time do you work?"

"They don't need me till late morning. That's fine. That's okay."

"Will you call later? Can we talk about things?"

Because she sounds as though her heart is not in it, I hang up, call back a minute later remembering that she is giving me a second chance. "Do you know where I am?" I ask. "In Duluth. I dreamt of you last night."

"When are you coming back? *Where* are you?"

"A long way from Bullfrog Country."

"How far? The Arctic Circle? What's life like up there?"

"I don't know yet. I've been in the motel room. You can see on the Internet where I am playing tonight. Look up Wade Stadium in the Northwoods League. I am lonely here."

"Do you remember what you said about marrying?"

This I cannot respond to with a game pending. When I can get no more out of her, I hang up for good.

"What'd she say?" asks Jason, suddenly interested in my business. "You ever going to marry her?"

"She works at eleven this morning. I bet right now she's changing cable channels and running a fingernail against her thumbnail to see whether the nail is smooth. I picture her looking out the window toward the Arctic Circle, putting off doing the dishes her Ma is nagging her about." (I cannot know *what* she is thinking, however. Does she brag about me? Does she say, "My boyfriend, Matt Folner, is a ballplayer?" Does she forget about my important baseball career, my improving my swing in the league, and think only of my saying yes to the question of marriage?)

I want to tell Jason what I tell everyone, but he is not in the mood. He is looking for something, his wallet or something. Whenever I narrate to others the thing I want to tell him, it is hard to stop, for telling it, I feel good. I have told all my friends and teammates in Oskaloosa how Becky was brushing her hair. It is the good Iowa color of gold. I have told everyone she had on a black sweater, blue jeans. Nervously, I had said such things that time as would make mature people laugh, such as, "I am a ballplayer, Becky." I then said,

"You are beautiful. You have green eyes."

"They're not green," she said.

"I'm eighteen," I told her, meaning I was old for this to be the first time.

"I was sixteen my first time."

"When?"

"I don't remember that," she said.

She didn't explain the mystery and meaning of how you could not know when you were sixteen. She turned from the mirror. I told her I wasn't sure what to do next.

"I am not sure either," she'd said.

We agreed to be certain of one thing—to do whatever we wanted. It didn't take long once I began what I, a Bullfrog, had hoped to do. When I was finished, I thought, This is what every man waits for. *Every* man. Then she was crying.

Afterwards, I said, "There is nothing wrong with crying."

"But how can you love someone who has small breasts?" she asked. It was like she was constantly devastated by this. She was as honest as anyone had ever been with me. "What if I'm pregnant?" she asked.

To get her mind off of things, I said, "You'll laugh if I tell you something."

"I won't laugh. You could laugh at me." Pulling a T-shirt on to hide herself, she asked, "What are you keeping from me?"

This is when I narrated the story of seeing an ad in the back of the newspapers you buy in the checkout lanes of supermarkets. I'd ordered a product from one of them. The ad had read, "LUCK BAD? Send for LUCKY POWDER. Lucky number in each pack, too. Sprinkle Good Luck Powder in shoes. Check number! Win Big! Enclose $5.00 plus stamped self-addressed envelope." I didn't care about winning, if there even was a prize. When the powder came, I sprinkled a little in each shoe. "And look," I said to her, "I got what I wanted." This is what she needed to know: that what we did came from love and good luck.

"Can I tell you something, Jason?" I ask when we are preparing to leave for our late lunch, then for the ballpark at Thirty-Fifth Avenue West and First Street.

"Sure," he says. Having found his wallet, he is willing to listen.

"A month ago I told my friends about the first time I was with Becky. They said, 'After she does it, it's nothing new for her to cry about her looks'—as if these guys knew about her. Can I tell you something else? I have had a dream of birds."

"Forget about birds. Why do you think all the time? Doesn't your brain get tired?"

"I have dreams of the type because when I saw our schedule I knew we were playing in the far north of Minnesota and in the south of Ontario when we play Thunder Bay late in the season. They are white birds with gray or black wings I dream about. Since the first of the dreams, I have located their picture on Wikipedia. Say there are one hundred of them in a tree, these northern birds. The tree shimmers. The snow buntings whir. They look like leaves of snow. They come down from the arctic and subarctic in winter. So many are in a flock that you cannot see what stands in the distance behind the tree of the snow buntings. 'Gregarious in the highest degree,' one place says, 'the vast, white flocks obscure the skies as they tower above weed fields from which they arise, whirling and circling, making a noise with their wings like the rushing of the wind.' My girlfriend is the answer to my prayers," I say to Jason who is more interested in what he is going to order at Perkins than in what I have to say about the white birds.

"You should forget about her. I'm hungry."

"You're right. I have to tell you, though—I know I sound stupid talking like this. I am gregarious like the snow buntings of the north. I also want to be polite in narrating it about Becky and me. I can't stop telling people. What's wrong with me?"

"You're in love. But I need a break. Let me eat in peace when we go."

I feel better when the story of my longing has been told. I feel closer to Becky by talking about her. The good feeling lasts an hour or two. I tell him Becky found out. "You told all of our secrets. How could you tell everyone we know?" she'd asked me on the day I'd gotten two triples against Buena Vista College.

"Now I know the secrets," Jason says over his omelet.

"It's not funny. Becky went three weeks where she wouldn't see me. I started losing weight, my batting average dropped. All because of my big mouth. When I call, she still does not say much. 'I am going to be honest and never lie to my parents or to myself again,' she has told me. This was toward the end of the college season. Sometimes I called her house. Mrs. Osterholm would say, 'She's gone out.'

"'Where?'

"'Honestly, I don't know. Is there something going on in town?'

"My parents would say, 'You're not acting right. What's gotten into you? Let's get back on track.'

"'I will,' I said. And I have."

When I ask Jason about the intimacy stuff he enjoys with his girlfriend—does she cry out? does she say things to him when they make love?—he will not answer.

I myself quiet down as we near the ballpark. When I see walls surrounding old sanctuaries of the sport and green roofs above grandstands and light standards rising into a blue afternoon, and when I feel and smell the warm, scented breeze, I get emotional in my heart as much as I would seeing Becky Osterholm, who I love as much as baseball. I could not choose between them, for both mean something to me. One is the promise of the good things of spring, the fresh outfield grass, the voice from a pressbox saying, "Batting fifth, left fielder Matt Folner." The other is the promise of her perfume and her small breasts and her honesty.

All manner of things bloom on a warm Minnesota afternoon. A botany major, Jason Spagnolli distinguishes for me between the flowers in peoples' yards. When we turn the corner outside the high stadium walls that are made of bricks salvaged from a street repair project in the 1940s, I see in the distance the ore dock he remembers from last season. At Wade Stadium, there have been many last seasons from when it was a minor league park for the Cardinals, White Sox, and Tigers. Surely someone from Iowa played here, missed his girl, fought through loneliness, went on to become famous, then returned to Mount Vernon, Cedar Falls, or Troy Mills on the Wapsipinicon River. Some old Iowa fellow must have played here once. Roaming left field, dreaming of the big leagues, he also would think of Pella, Ottumwa, or some other Iowa town he loved ten or twelve hours south of here.

From the Super 8, the guys have ridden the short distance on the bus, which is parked in the stadium lot. Jason and I do not bother with the players' entrance. When we walk through the main gate, we see concession stands, vendors preparing for work. To graduate from William Penn College, home of the Statesmen, then to sign a pro contract and be famous around Oskaloosa, I have my work cut out for me. Going up the runway on the third base side, we gaze out at the paradise where we will spend two evenings representing the honor of the Green Bay Bullfrogs. The June breeze blows through the crown of trees beyond the right field wall.

"I will give you Lucky Powder when we change into our uniforms and take the field," I tell him. I decide that toward season's end, dying from loneliness, I will also give Coach Boyd Barton a packet of Lucky Powder and tell him about Becky. I wonder whether Coach will say: "You were all right, Folner, except for your talking. Nevertheless, I will tell the Rangers and Phillies to keep an eye on you. Go back to wherever you're from remembering what you've learned here. But one thing—cut back on the talk. Do this and I'll give you a big buildup."

I have to talk. I can't stop. I am lonely, I think as I relax beside the batting cage awaiting batting practice. Why is it that nothing is said when I call Becky? We do not speak fifteen words. Yet in thousands of words I have told my buddies about the moment when the woman takes the man—if it is his first time—and directs him to the secret place he is meant to go. In hundreds of words I have told everyone she scratches her nails into me as if never wanting to let go. I have told in more words how, when Becky and I are loving each other, she bites my arm, grabs my hair. My last time with her in bed I had on a Bullfrogs cap to keep her from doing this. Why is it wrong telling what men and women do, and that, at age eighteen, I have entered the secret club? My parents do not know how far we've gone.

The late spring twilight represents for me the things that could be in life. No sadder time of day exists than when the shadows of a ballpark's light standards fall on the green outfields of America. I will loosen my arm with throws from left. I will take fungoes off of the bat of our assistant coach. I will examine left field as though examining Becky's body. Even in full daylight, there are hazards. In Iowa we left open her bedroom window to hear if her mom or dad drove up. We went in her car to the edge of the cornfield to be alone. Even there someone would come by. In ballparks you can collide with the bullpen fence, the light standards. You can crash into the outfield wall or trip on the turf in daytime. At night, a park's lights do not illuminate foul territory very well. Sometimes I have to chase fly balls into hazardous places. Unlike a center fielder flanked by players, I, Matt, am alone, vulnerable.

I remember early on this evening to glide on the balls of my feet when tracking a fly ball, to position myself behind where it comes down so as to step toward it for the quick throw to second, third, or home. Everyone will wait as the ball descends to the left fielder from Oskaloosa. The coach has confidence in me. He has his eye on me for the big leagues. Over the noise, the excitement of fans, the chatter of players, the P.A. system blaring music through the stadium, I hear Coach Barton yelling, "How you gonna get back, Spagnolli?" as he drills a hard shot Jason's way during infield practice.

When we're in the dugout, I say, "Here." I hand Jason an extra packet of powder. This results in a base hit. On my first time up, I bounce a single through the same place in the infield as he does. On first base, I remind myself: When you take a lead, don't lean toward second. Watch the pitcher's heel on the rubber to see if he's throwing to first. When you run, cross left leg over right, pivot, don't shuffle. Thus prepared, I free my mind to meditate on Becky.

The powder brings us further success when Jason makes a key put out to end the third. Two innings later when the public address announcer announces me as the next batter, we are getting shut out 4-0, but I respond with a clutch double. "I do it for you, Becky," I whisper as I round second and trot back to the bag. "It's dark now down in Iowa. I bet you are going somewhere with your friends."

During the sixth inning, the dew gets heavy on the grass. I have made several put outs in fair territory. We have plenty of at bats left. We have the heart of the order coming up. We have Matt Folner. But I guess I have only so much good luck, for in the seventh, I find out too late I should have bought new spikes before I left Oskaloosa. Having gone through a college season, including the early spring trip to Florida for twelve games, my spikes have a quarter-inch of steel left on them. Pivoting toward the foul line, Lucky Powder guiding every step, but with no traction, I slip chasing a line drive. In the moment I sprawl on the wet grass before rising, I think of her. I am dazed how everything slips away as the ball rolls to the warning track, bouncing into the shadows of foul territory before I retrieve it and gun it to Jason for the relay.

On the first night after my nineteenth birthday (and after three runs score), I realize you cannot keep things in the field of play forever. A lesson is written here.

In the eighth, I have another try at Duluth Huskies' pitching. I am three-for-three tonight. When I strike out, I watch down the third base line as shadows edge in from foul territory.

"Why didn't you swing?" Jason asks on our way onto the field for the bottom of the inning. I say nothing. Under the stadium lights with the scent of apple tree blossoms, lilacs, and new grass surrounding us in this cool and lovely place, I look at the sky, at heaven. A train is moving out along the ore dock.

"Why didn't you?" he asks again, thinking I didn't hear. But I am speechless. How do I tell him I have never loved a game or a woman so much? I don't know which counts for more, the game or the girl whose dad runs the insurance agency back home.

"I couldn't, I couldn't swing," I say. I know it in my heart.

It wasn't that their pitcher had tied me up when I was thinking fastball and he threw me a curve, or that, behind by so much, I'd given up. I am not sure if why I didn't swing had to do with the game at all. Maybe it concerned the long trip from Green Bay to a beautiful, unfamiliar place south of the Arctic Circle. Maybe it concerned how I woke up today and what we had for lunch and how we'd walked to the ballpark and the twilight of earlier and the blooming of every flower, bush, and tree in the late northern spring. Or maybe it had to do with the promise of what an Iowa summer will bring me if I quit the Bullfrogs and head home after more than a week away. I'd get there tomorrow.

This evening the beauty of everything in life—the big lake nearby, the Northwoods League, the girl I love, the infield dust, the game itself—all of these things prove too much. By the top of the ninth, I understand there is only one sure place for Matt Folner in this world of doubt, strife, and sorrow. It will be on a baseball diamond—not only this one in Duluth, but on every diamond in any league I play in. As I make my way in the game all the way to the majors, I will shape these diamonds into hearts of love and longing for Becky Osterholm.

Your Hit Parade

"If Mel Torme is 'The Velvet Fog,' shouldn't I at least be 'The Elegant Mist'? Surveys indicate that even during station identification, which this is, you enjoy hearing my radio voice. From the studio at the antenna farm, I, Luther Craft (formerly Larry Krabenhoff), read you news, weather, commercials. I take requests, introduce singers, bands. On this, *The Night Train Show,* you want to hear Julie London, Duke Ellington, Johnny Mathis, Jimmy Dorsey, Glen Gray and His Casa Loma Orchestra, Vic Damone, other soothing voices and bands. Anything from the '40s and '50s. Frankie Laine, Etta James, Percy Faith, Nat 'King' Cole.

"Demographics show that Superior, Wisconsin, needs an 'easy listening' station, that many of you are old and tired. In our station's survey, sixty percent of you describe yourselves as 'Young Old Timers.' Forty percent of you receive Meals on Wheels. Twenty-two percent visit senior citizen centers at least twice weekly for companionship. Five percent play Canasta at the centers.

"Hey, I'm a senior citizen. You and I, we don't need demographic surveys to know we're oldsters who like things done right. I am a voice broadcasting from an old town who knows our music is best.

"Golden Agers, 1390 AM is the place for you. *The Night Train*

Show. That hint of raspiness in my voice suggests I've been around. I used to work at KSAD-Radio in these Twin Ports of Superior-Duluth, where our playlist consisted of sad songs. Roy Orbison's 'Crying,' Elvis's 'Kentucky Rain,' Johnny Ray's 'The Little White Cloud that Cried'—mainly songs from the early-to-mid rock era.

"I'm glad I made the switch to the easy listening format at 1390. This low, confident voice assures you when autumn leaves start to fall, we'll have these moments to remember. It assures you, young at heart 1390 listeners, that 'You're sure to survive to a hundred and five, if you're young at heart.' (Remember *that* catchy Sinatra lyric?) Here I am to tell you love is a many splendored thing, 'so if she's the one,' as Pat Boone reminds us, 'don't let her slip away.' You won't slip away from me, dear friends. There may be no one else for you but Luther.

"At 3 a.m., I hope I'm easy to listen to when I confess these personal matters. It's you and me: Lute hugging the mic, speaking to you one on one, to your heart alone. I have love for each of you. Love for you on East Third Street all by yourself. Can't sleep tonight?—I have love for you in the downstairs apartment on North Seventeenth and for you, lonely lady, on South Tower Avenue. You're still a *Night Train* fan, aren't you? I need you, you know. I bet your lights are on. You're broken-hearted over the fellow who left you. Despite what you say—that he was no good—you cry yourself to sleep. Sometimes you hum the *Moulin Rouge* theme from that wonderful movie John Huston directed with Jose Ferrer and Zsa Zsa in '52. Was that the song you said, dear lady? Or was it 'Theme from *A Summer Place*?' Call me tonight. Let me know. I've been waiting to hear from you. I forgot the title you once told me, but I haven't forgotten you in your sadness, how your mother and you saw the movie when you were young. You sat in the enclosed smoking loge upstairs at the Superior Theater in East End. The wide glass window let you see the show while it kept your mother's cigarette smoke from drifting downstairs. Half a century later, you watch *Moulin Rouge* or *A Summer Place* on the VCR that your ex-lover allowed you to keep when he returned to his wife—a payoff for your broken heart after loving him.

"I'm broken hearted, too. I told you my wife pulled out on me twenty years ago when I was still at KSAD. I was forty-eight then. That was the topic of last week's *Night Train Show*: my disastrous marriage. Topics of the preceding weeks were a person's faith in God and the joys of friendship for the senior citizen living in Superior, Wisconsin. Tonight's topic is the story of my sister's piano career.

"At 3 a.m. this night of a blue moon, the world is ours, dear listeners. We'll grow old together a song at a time at 1390. Here's an item to grow old by: did you know a 'blue moon' has nothing to do with color, but with a coincidence that occurs when two full moons appear in the same month. This happens infrequently, which is why you hear the phrase 'once in a blue moon.'

"Tonight from the studio at the antenna farm where twenty antennas beam every local radio and TV stations' signal, give me fifteen minutes. Then we'll have Rosemary Clooney, Glenn Miller, Harry James, Sinatra again. If you listen, I'll give you alone my heart in the middle of this night of a blue moon. You've been so good I'll offer you a very lonely, personal view of Luther. Please call, listener from the past whose song I forgot. At night on the radio, we'll dream together. We'll forget the present, forget what the Twin Ports and America have become in 2007. Are movies good these days? I don't go to them. Before work last night, I watched five minutes of TV. An anorexic girl in a bikini balanced plates, saucers, and a teacup on the end of a stick while an emcee told her she could join the 'tribal council.' What does it mean, this and the iPods, MP3 players, and HGH Major League Baseball players insist they don't use? When daylight comes, do you get the feeling, Golden Agers, that we don't belong, we don't understand America?

"Something's off in the new century. I don't want it. I get home at seven in the morning. I draw the blinds, put on a pot of coffee, play my 45's and 78's. I live in the darkness of the modern world remembering TWIRP dances at East High, Superior Blues minor league baseball, 'Catman' Walker, the WEBC deejay.

"Duluth was a great city back then, too. You know that, 1390's Duluth listeners. What a journey for us over the Arrowhead or Interstate bridge from Superior. When ore and grain boats approached the bridges on the St. Louis River estuary, the bridges' center spans lifted or swung out; the traffic stopped high up there. Buses, trucks, and automobiles sometimes had to wait a half hour. Duluth had a small amusement park on Minnesota Point. You could see it from up on the Interstate Bridge. The merry-go-round, the concession stand, miles of summer beaches—in the distance 'red sails in the sunset.' Life was quiet. Nothing extreme then in Superior-Duluth. To promote yourself during today's Apocalypse, you have to wear black, contort your body when you swagger, say 'yo' to everything, send hand signals to your 'homey.' This will establish you as the Man, establish that you are from the 'hood, though Superior has no bad neighborhoods so I don't know which 'hood this could be. If you're young, it's important to be extreme, to be alienated, important to wear 'bling,' to 'Do the Dew.' I'm talking about white kids. It's not for me to speak of anyone else. They make up 99.9 percent of Superior's youth. Some of them despise their color. They want to leave the split-level or the historic home overlooking Hammond or Washington park to live in an East St. Louis tenement. Despite his swagger, a boy from Superior wouldn't last a minute down there. East St. Louis is someone else's problem.

"I'm pounded from dreams, sometimes, by cars going by—kids named Michalski, Anderson, and Swenson playing hop-hip or hop, skip, and a-jump music on their radio. What's appealing about AK-47s and drugs? Sometimes these kids park ouside the station, radios thumping, blasting. I lock the gate at night. On cell phones, they call Luther in the studio. They say, 'Yo, why you dissin' my music, why you dissin' Fi'ty Cent and Jay-Z?' They suck the spirit from life, menace me—menace us, good listeners—with woofers, subwoofers, foul language. Sweatshirt hoods hide their faces. Let's say there are eighty or ninety such kids in the city. You see them about. Their great-grandparents attend Concordia Lutheran, St. Alban the Martyr.

Probably they are my listeners. Probably one of them is tuned in tonight. I know you're sick of what you see, Great-grandparents.

"We must stick together. We can do this on the radio at night. We can do it another way by banding together to fight for our rights and our safety. We will draw the blinds at home, watch reruns of *Wagon Train*. Golden Agers, we'll make a world out of the one left behind. What we had in the '40s and '50s was precious. I'm serious. This is my plan: I advocate for a life lived in the twilight of the past. It was good then. 'Heavenly shades of night are falling. It's twilight time.' Why give this up? Why abandon Kathryn Grayson and Howard Keel in *Show Boat* or Gene Kelly in *Singin' in the Rain*? Why not form special interest groups where we treat ourselves differently from the way AARP does? Our groups will specialize in what twilight really offers—the notion that our lives have been fulfilled, the notion that a day is almost done. We will be local. We will be locally run. No AARP for us.

"I am, you know, for Greer Garson and Maureen O'Hara on the screen; for dinners with the family gathered round (if the kids aren't there, imagine how it was when they were); for a deemphasis on reality TV and so-called 'news' shows; for a reemphasis on old movies and easy listening. I propose the clubs we form spend afternoons enjoying yearbooks from Superior's and Duluth's high schools, old newspapers, too. Once a week someone can report on what happened in the Twin Ports on January 6, 1947, on August 1, 1950, on October 18, 1953. Cloquet, Proctor, and Two Harbors Golden Agers, we'll reminisce about your glory days. During our meetings at area Drop-In Centers, we can listen to The Mills Brothers, The Inkspots, The Lettermen. We can dance and sing till 'deep purple falls over sleepy garden walls.' We'll call ourselves 'The Gold Club,' 'The Silver Club,' 'Traditions' maybe. The point is we must be deliberate. Members must agree the past is better, and we must want to make the past the present. We'll live in the velvet fog of our youth. Call Luther. Call him tonight to tell him we can succeed by hiding out in memory. At my age, sixty-something years young, I have many,

many memories.

"It's no big deal about my sister, Maria. At 3:07 a.m., she's someone to talk about. Three years older than me, she lives in Phoenix, Sun City actually, with her husband. In that golden place, she's probably gotten beyond the bad spot in her life some fifty-odd years ago. Sorrow recalled often will make you want to stop living. That's my job, to get your mind off of things at 3:09 this morning. 'Primrose Lane, life's a holiday on Primrose Lane.' Give me ten minutes, and I'll get you back to the music of your life.

"Maria had a chance to be on *Jack Paar*. At the Superior Theater talent show, the first prize was a trip to Milwaukee where, we were told, a judge would choose the person who'd be on Mr. Paar's program in New York City. I was in eighth grade. I never attended one talent show. That's how strict our dad was. Movies playing before the talent show—things like *Al Capone* or Jane Russell in *The Outlaw*—were almost always in the 'Morally Objectionable' category on the list we followed in the *Our Sunday Visitor*, so I couldn't go to them. I know this: kids who tap-danced or made hand silhouettes and funny noises or performed magic tricks didn't get past the first night of the competition. Those who played bebop or Fats Domino had a chance because the place would be packed with high schoolers to cheer them on. Who'd applaud a tap-dancing eighth-grader from Cooper School?

"I don't remember adults entering the talent competition. Refresh me on this point. It's never too late at night or too early in the morning to telephone your faithful Luther. *Moulin Rouge* lady, I want to hear from you. It isn't All Soul's Night, but May 31, a blue moon night. Pretend it is All Soul's, though, because it's just your heart and mine. My soul is lonely. I have nothing awaiting me at home but old songs and a Mercury AG 4100 hi-fi from 1960 to spin them on, not even a console but a portable that 'plays all records, sizes, and speeds—monaural or stereo.'

"Maria Krabenhoff, what a lovely name to say over the radio. 'Maria, I just met a girl named Ma-ri-a.' Somehow, playing

'Malaguena' and 'Claire de Lune' on the piano, she got through the month of preliminary competition. When Maria, a winner, came in with my parents at eleven o'clock, she'd be smiling. Out of gratitude to the theater manager, they'd stayed for the double feature. She was a sophomore. As far as my parents were concerned, she could see movies that were Morally Objectionable in Part if she advanced to the next week.

"'Was it as exciting as ever tonight?' Ma'd ask about the performance.

"'Jack Paar's still on,' Dad would say, opening a bottle of beer at the kitchen table.

"'I want to be on *Your Hit Parade*. I could accompany Snooky Lanson on 'This Ol' House' and Gisèle MacKenzie on 'Canadian Sunset,' Maria would say. Bustling about in the outfit she'd worn at her command performance at the Superior Theater, she must have thought she was in Vienna or Paris.

"'You're on your way. Jack Paar's waiting,' Dad would say, having another beer, opening one for my mother.

"WEBC 560 broadcast the final two Fridays live. Figuring she couldn't win with the kind of music her piano teacher encouraged her to play, I still listened—mainly to hear someone perform a fast song with a beat. No one cares about classical music; Maria had no chance to win, my friends and I figured. We were pulling for a band from the North End called Ronnie Carl and the Roulettes.

"Our family and our relatives belonged as much to the East End neighborhood as we did to St. Francis Xavier Church. My parents bought groceries here, had our shoes fixed here, went to the dimestore or Lederman's Clothing Store here. Because of their talented daughter, Mr. and Mrs. Krabenhoff were suddenly important. This was '57. No wonder the excitement about my sister. There was no cable TV, no multiplex theaters, no X-treme games. When Maria got through the semifinal night, Ma asked people in the bakery to come to the one remaining talent show to support her. My dad bought rounds for the guys at Stranko's Tavern, then shifted his base of operations across the street to Howard's Tavern, then down to Nadolski's. My uncles and aunts lobbied their friends on Maria's behalf. To see them acting like this, and Dad drinking so much because he couldn't handle the excitement, was odd, for they were mainly quiet people who stayed out of the limelight. Maria's success was now my parents' and my relatives' success. I knew this is when—tonight in 2007—I'd start to feel bad, at this moment. I knew it. Stay tuned. We've got a commercial break—

"Now that I've told you to pre-buy oil and propane from Como Oil for next year's heating season, I can't wait to give you the story. Something's hidden in my heart. What have I got to lament? I ask those of you tuned in at 3:18 a.m. of a person's life. Maybe I should lament that when people leave, I am lost. When I sign off from you, good listeners, I'm lost. My wife left. Did I tell you? I did? Yes, I forgot. When I look in the mirror in the living room at home, I see a radio personality who got the future he deserved. No one but Luther rides the Night Train. I am The Moonlight Gambler Frankie Laine told you about.

"When you've been in radio this long, in order to rest, you sometimes need a commercial break or a news break at the top of the hour when we go to the network. On this special night with Luther, I need no breaks, however. Are you out there? Are you with me? I don't mean you with your music shaking the earth outside the gate.

"In '57, I got jealous of my sister. If she persisted in playing classical music, then none of the kids in eighth grade—me included—wanted her winning. No one at East High School wanted Maria to win, I bet. My friends and I thought it was a setup between the theater manager and the grown-ups to choose her the winner. The adults believed my mature sister's success would set a good example for the rest of us and that's why they came out on the last night of the talent competition—or so we figured. My buddies and I were wrong about the setup, which at least wasn't an inside job as far as the manager was concerned. He had nothing to do with fixing the show. His job was to help promote a contest that was run by some guy from outside of town, a guy we heard was a talent scout.

"The week before the big night, I started getting dirty looks from kids who wanted Ronnie Carl and the Roulettes to win. 'Why's she wrecking it for us?' they'd ask me at school or when I was going somewhere.

"I told them I'd disown her if she won. I had a lot of reasons to be angry. Because I was related to Maria Krabenhoff, the musician, there was my reputation to worry about. Everything in the house always revolved around my sister with her honey blond hair, her green eyes, her long fingers racing over the keyboard. Her hands flew in the air when she played. You were reminded of Liberace.

"Fifty-some years later, I can tell you she didn't stand a chance. After what Ronnie Carl and the Roulettes played, Liberace performing 'The Warsaw Concerto' couldn't have won. Maybe its being the first Friday in Lent had something to do with how things turned out. Perhaps that year, on March 8, God descended over a theater that stood within sight of a steeple. Something holy happened a block from St. Francis.

"For a week she'd practiced at school, so I had no idea what she'd be playing. Ear to the radio, I was excited after hearing the Roulettes, excited that nobody could beat them. Then someone introduced Maria. I heard kids boo. She coughed twice, I suppose out of nervousness, then started Schubert's 'Ave Maria,' and I think people were so moved and affected by the selection that no one applauded, but when they did, it kept on for four full minutes on a Friday night. The roses she won (Ronnie Carl presented them to her) ended up in a cut glass vase next to the Virgin's statue on our dining room table.

"When my sister and my mother left for Milwaukee, kids were hanging around the neighbor's front porch watching everything at our house. Mr. Moniak would drive them to the train station while my dad was at work. After bringing out the suitcases, I beat it back inside the house. Ma looked at the downstairs picture window, then at my room upstairs to see why I wasn't coming to say goodbye. The front of the gray-shingled house must have seemed as blank to my mother as Maria's face at that moment: My sister couldn't believe she was a star. Many East Enders had donated money for the trip. All expenses would be paid by the sponsor when they arrived in Milwaukee.

"To avoid the kids who'd watched her leave in Moniak's car, I slipped out the back door and went down the alley to the drugstore, which, for a few days, had had stickers in the window advertising aspirin, cough syrup, pills, toothpaste, shaving cream—all for a penny if you bought one for the regular price. From 2 to 4 p.m., a disk jockey was broadcasting live the way we occasionally do today from Devinck Motors. When a song went out, he'd chat with customers. After the record ended, he'd go live over the air again advertising the sale in 'Friendly East End.'

"A few grown-ups stood around watching when I got there. Two or three women from church busied themselves at the greeting card rack. Some high schoolers were walking in. When I looked up from the comic book I was examining, I saw my future in Gerry 'Catman' Walker, who looked different, cooler, than I'd expected him to. Someone had pointed me out to him as the brother of a soon-to-be New York celebrity.

"'Come on over,' he said. 'Do you want to make a request?'

"Pointing to the record he had playing on the turntable, he waited for it to end, then put down another record. Turning on the mic, he said, 'This one goes out for Maria Krabenhoff.' 'That's the name, right? She won the talent show?' he asked me off-mic, then he held the microphone toward me. 'What's next for our listeners' enjoyment?' He wanted me to tell the radio audience what I'd requested.

"I stuttered. I was so nervous I asked him to say what it was, but 'Catman' Walker laughed and shook his head at me until, gathering strength, I whispered 'Blue Moon,' and for the three minutes it played, I was famous at a one-cent sale.

"My effort wasn't worth a penny. There was no talent

competition, no judge, no hotel reservations in downtown Milwaukee. We'd been set up by a stranger who'd convinced the theater manager, the entire neighborhood and city, to trust him, then left with two months of talent show money, probably a thousand dollars. They never caught him. You might remember reading about it in the paper.

"That night in a Milwaukee hotel after she found out there'd be no *Jack Paar Show*, I wonder how Maria got through her sorrow. Knowing the embarrassment awaiting them at home, what could Ma have told her? Night after night from this area of broadcast antennas reddening the night sky with fires that may never be extinguished, I play the songs of memory, recall the past, the losses, the hurt. Can you hear me, Maria? In the studio or in the house where we grew up and where I live alone, I wonder every night about you and about God's presence in our lives. Why did this happen to you? Why did I act as I did? When you came home, I pretended to my friends you'd suffered a reverse divine intervention for playing what you'd played to keep Rockin' Ronnie Carl from going to Milwaukee. I cannot forget the things I did, 1390 listeners. How do you forget the music that haunts you?

"I won't pretend to be what I'm not. You know me too well. Let me quote this one Bible verse, however, for I am generally not a holy man. In Numbers, when Aaron and Miriam grow jealous of Moses, he intercedes with the Lord to cure her of her 'white leprosy,' a mild punishment. The Lord says to him, 'Suppose her father had spit in her face, would she not hide in shame for seven days?' Maria, too, had been shamed. My parents had been shamed by what happened. The greatest shame was mine, I've seen over the years. They were innocent. I wasn't. I'd hated her for a time.

"Maria returned to East High, but it was hell there for her. Kids laughed and talked about her. My parents didn't know how to give back the quarters and dimes people had contributed for the trip. The bank had given ten dollars; Art Haugen at the drugstore ten; St. Francis Church fifteen.

"My mother kept us going by figuring a way out of the embarrassment of owing anyone anything. She worked hard around the neighborhood, baked for people, did favors for them. Dad stopped drinking. Maria got through the school year, but quit practicing the piano. Why should she have hidden in shame when she'd done nothing wrong? I was the one who should have been punished for what, like Aaron and Miriam, I'd done behind my sister's back by ridiculing her.

"In time, Maria graduated, left home to work. I went in the service, kicked about for a year or two afterward, but I could never get the East End neighborhood out of my mind. When I returned home from my travels, I thought about selling insurance with my cousin, the American Family agent. But how could I insure others when I never insured myself? Where do you buy a policy against regret?

"With Maria out west, I grow lonely in the house where we grew up. Outside on the street, I hear car speakers pounding rap music, hip-hop. Things were better back then—no school shootings, no ear-splitting music. Here in the 1390 studio tonight, I think of the uninsured of long ago. Antennas beam signals to the sky, always outward, always away. Tonight I have you with me to hear these transmissions from the heart. We go inward tonight, deep into the place where we try to make amends.

"At 3:26, let me tell you the signals of people from back then—Gerry 'Catman' Walker of one-cent sale fame, my parents, my aunts and uncles—come in clearly everyday. Maria's signal I never hear, though. Never. Before taking the trip so many years ago that changed her life, I wonder if she heard my request. I wonder if she is listening tonight. This next song is for you, Beloved Sister, so far away. And it's for you, *Moulin Rouge* lady. And for the rest of you 1390 listeners. Jo Stafford's 'Blue Moon.' I'll be quiet now and listen."

Wesolewski, Hedwig
Room 301

To someone coming to town in the rain that bedevils the coast, the $20 per night room rate is agreeable. Drying their tears on this damp night, the broken-hearted shake their coats on the worn carpeting and ask quietly whether a hotel room is available to them. The blue neon sign adds to their hopelessness. The "I" is burned out. HOTEL CHOP N HOTEL CHOP N, it reads.

"How long will your stay be?" I inquire from behind the reservation desk. A hotelier for thirty years, I am never surprised by the appearance of the depressed or lonely.

"Forever," they say. "Someone has hurt me so bad I'll have to stay forever."

The melancholy foghorn signals ships beyond the piers, the rain drifts down. There they stand with nowhere to go, explaining over and over, "Someone I love hurt me." Their glum faces look blue from the sign.

"Good, sir, then I'll see what we have for you. I'll write in the guest register, 'Will stay here forever.'"

"It might take a little longer to get over her, maybe twice as long as that," they tell me.

"And what else is causing the gentleman's sorrow this rainy

night? Our weather? His unanswered prayers? His hopelessness caused by financial ruin?" Sometimes they nod yes to the questions. They dry their tears. They take out a prayer book that's done them no good. They open their coats and jackets, point imploringly to their hearts, say, "This is all of it I have left. I am nearly heart less." I recall a visitor unbuttoning his shirt to expose the heart tattooed on his chest. A surgery scar zigzagged through it, making the tattoo look stitched together. Right before my eyes, the physical misery of a heart surgery blended with the emotional misery of a broken heart.

Do you remember Arthur Dimmesdale? Alone at midnight in his room, "gnawed and tortured by some black trouble of the soul," he brands his chest in Hawthorne's lovely book. He would fit in here. Do you remember the Lord Jesus Christ, how His heart is broken at Gethsemane? He belongs here. Do you remember His mother in her pain? In which room is she? Nothing but pain and sorrow at the Hotel Chopin.

The folk dancers aren't crying when they arrive. With the fog and rain, this would be too much for me, a whole troupe of crying dancers. If any weep privately, it's from knowing they'll be overworked. For eight hours a day, they are going to practice at the auditorium nearby, perform for the public in late April, then rent a new bus for a cross-country tour. Mazowsza, I think is their name—no, not Mazowsza, Zgoda Dance Troupe of Eastern Europe.

For a month, I have been preparing. Apologizing to the consumptives on the third and fourth floors for the disturbance, I have taped on each door a photocopied sheet of rules. WHEN THE DANCERS ARRIVE: NO WASHING YOUR FEET IN THE BIDET; NO WAILING OR KEENING AFTER MIDNIGHT; NO WEEPING IN FULL VIEW OF THEM; NO ASKING GUESTS ABOUT THEIR OWN POSSIBLE HEARTACHES. In the hallway I have hung garlands of ivy, placed rose-colored shades over the yellow lightbulbs, though perhaps scarlet shades would have been better. Downstairs in the lobby, I've swept chairs with a whisk broom, scraped a spot from one, dried a young man's tears from another.

I've been in the hospitality trade long enough to know the manager of a dancing troupe might not care for my fussiness. His job being to cut costs, which explains why he lodges his troupe at the Hotel Chopin, he'll notice only casually the bridge lights over the canal shading the sides of the building blue or the look of the shabby lobby I've tried improving with potted palms and an artificial fountain.

When the bus rolls in, parking on Lake Avenue, I check my appearance in the window. This is an opportunity for a hotelier who hasn't done well in life. As the bus door opens, I look for a Mr. Boris Zukovsky, the manager who has written me with his room reservation needs. Speaking of the dismal weather, holding an umbrella over him, I escort him indoors. Resuming my public face behind the reservation desk, I assign his dancers—Irina, Bruno, Dorota, Urszula, Nikolai—to their rooms. Sturdy Slavs, they stand dumbly waiting until the next five step up, then the next five.

Pleased how Mr. Zukovsky says "Thank you" in Russian or Polish when the first phase of our transaction is completed, I prepare a glass of tea back in the alcove. Selecting a tin of specialty crackers from the shelf, I tell myself I will have to purchase a samovar. As the water boils for tea, I hear something, a sigh perhaps. Shutting off the stove burner, brushing crumbs from my trousers, I pull aside the curtain.

"I have been lost," says a young woman. She appears sad, shy. Perhaps she is embarrassed by her accent. She looks at the desk, at the floor. Has Burl, the handyman, swept and mopped there? Does he do the job my superior asks him to? I have done more cleaning than Burl this week.

"Oh dear," I say when I check the guest register to see what is available. "You're a dancer without a home." (Before I remember the set of rules I've given my tenants to follow, I want to ask, Who of your thirty is the loneliest? Is it you, Hedwig? Is it Zukovsky, the manager?) "I have a single room to let, but it's on the third floor. You've come in late. It will have to do."

"Mr. Zukovsky will be notified I am in different place, not on second floor?" she asks.

"Yes," I tell her.

I give her the room I once slept in. From the radiator, paint is flaking. The framed picture of a winter scene on the wall hangs crookedly. There are a dresser with a dirty mirror and a bed with a coverlet that bears spots where an unsteady pensioner dropped his cough medicine. (Burl was to have cleaned this!) Beside the other piece of furniture in the room, the love seat, I place her bags. Like the hotel's namesake, I am a romantic. Mornings in my smoking jacket, I once sat semirecumbent in the love seat, listening to the great Chopin on the phonograph, staring at the harbor. I would read aloud LaMartine's "The Lake," Huysmans' *Au Reboir*, then observe the strollers on the avenue below.

"I hope you enjoy your room," I say bowing my way out.

Later, I cannot help writing her name. I remember how she'd stood opposite me, how I'd looked at her. When her head was bowed, I'd looked and looked for the longest time. In the guest register, I see the name again: Wesolewski, Hedwig Room 301.

In bed I think of her. Earlier this day, she seemed to know how life has been for me. Do a drawn face and dark circles under the eyes give away so much of the heart's losses? In my old room on my old mattress, she sinks into the shape my body has made. It is like my shape holds and comforts hers. Is she naked? Lonely? I have been naked on the mattress. She might be naked while I am at the reservation desk. I cannot take a chance on finding out. I have had trouble in the hospitality industry. I have bothered guests who didn't want to be bothered, and I can't risk another setback. Though a petty thief, I'd take nothing of value if I saw her naked.

Such intrusions of privacy as I would like to commit have happened against me in hotels. Through the thin walls came noises I misunderstood when I was young. Listening to them, wondering what they meant, I fretted, as I drifted in and out of sleep, whether the desk clerk would remember to wake me in time to catch the five a.m. train to Pittsburgh. In places like this, the staff did little to please. In unclean hotels with plugged toilets, no one cares about the night's lodgers. Say it is three a.m. in Cincinnati or Louisville. Say I am twenty years old, not my present age. The light tapping starts on the door. It is followed by the rustling of keys as the desk clerk slips in. Thinking I am asleep, he's come—dressed as a woman—to steal money, but realizing his mistake steals something more personal then leaves me blue. He is too strong for me to fight off. When I check out, he smirks. A trace of lipstick on his cheek, he asks whether I enjoyed my stay.

In other places, things have happened. Out of the fog, strangers have come to me. From doorfronts, they've strolled up. "Dark night," they whispered to start the conversation. By harbors of big cities—Baltimore, say—lonely intruders saw me in their matchglow, shed light on me, saw who I was, though no names were exchanged. Thank God I wasn't always lonely. In the Hotel Chopin, guests' rooms are to be held sacred, inviolate. Leave the lonely their due.

This is my hotel philosophy: A person taking a room, no matter how much he or she pays or whether her manager pays, deserves the special considerations a desk clerk and night manager can give, provided my ministrations do not violate her privacy. I want the place to be safe—distinctive, too, so guests remember how different we are from the Seaway Hotel or the Hotel d'Azure. With a dance troupe tucked away for the night, I tell Burl, "Get the ladder." Above the landing on the way to their floor, he screws a pulley into the ceiling according to my sketched plan. Working quietly, he threads thick twine over the pulley wheel, dropping one end to me. As Burl accompanies me with his end, I unroll twine from a ball. Walking from the landing to the lobby, we guide the twine high over the potted plants, over the leather couch, straight to the reservation desk, where awaits the *pièce de résistance*: a wicker basket I have used to carry fruit and bread. The ascent of the basket, a cable car of the air, is to be controlled by a crank. "Ha-ha, that's you—a crank, Harry," Burl says.

"No, Burl," I say. "For my lodgers' convenience, I can, with this system, sweep their letters, even their light packages, halfway to second floor. I aim the basket, put in materials, turn the crank, and off they go. An ingenious method of delivery, a parcel post. Don't you agree, Burl, it makes us special?"

"Can they send things back?"

"Do you mean unsolicited mail?"

"If they need something in their rooms, if they run out of soap, can they send a request?"

"Service is the aim of the hotel. I will crank away for them. Be certain of that."

To insure the privacy I have rarely enjoyed, I again warn my residents, including the handyman, to follow rules. NO DRAWING BROKEN HEARTS ON HOTEL STATIONERY. NO LEAVING DRAWINGS IN LOBBY! Most of the lodgers are too sick to draw. My upper floors are a tubercular ward. All I hear most days is the shuffling of the slippers of old men heading down hallways to the bathroom—this, or God save us, a blast of something from their lungs or from that foulest hole in the body. Their decrepitude notwithstanding, I have changed the locks on the second floor where the dancers are staying (this was a month ago) in case an old man, rooming with me for a year, has somehow gotten a key.

I sleep soundly this night. I am better in the morning. The dancers are out. They have arranged to take their breakfasts down the street, then go to practice, remaining until late afternoon, so the place is clear. It stays this way while I get my work done.

For two or three days, I do not see Hedwig Wesolewski, and though I've not forgotten her and my bed, I regain my composure. Funny how her looks have upset me, her blonde hair, her large, almond-shaped eyes, her uncertainty as she stood there. Perhaps Chopin felt this way about George Sand.

Because she has received no letters like the others, I stop going so carefully through the mail when it arrives, although after practice when they have relaxed, other dancers come to the second floor landing for mail. It is just in the nature of things that my comings and goings do not coincide with Hedwig Wesolewski's, I begin to think. Yet I watch for her, wonder how it is I've not seen her. It is foolish of me. What is she, after all, but a dancer with whom I've exchanged a few words on the way upstairs to her room? How I would love sending her mail by the pulley, how I'd love sleeping naked on the mattress her shape has changed for me.

When I see her again, she smiles and waves. Unable to move, I stand beside the desk, saying something to her about the fog and how she mustn't fear for her privacy. Too excited to do much else, knowing I am alone now that she is in her room, I keep along with my work. What else is there to do? If I can get Burl to spell me, I'll go out walking, spend an hour at the video theater annoying men dreaming their loneliness away in the peepshows. "Get out of here," they almost always say when I join them in their privacy.

Returning to the Hotel Chopin, I shudder to think the evening is here. I find myself polishing the brass fixtures on the third floor. When I do not see Hedwig, I grow anxious. She has probably taken a lover. For a moment, I hate living here. Hotels isolate people. Who but an isolated man lodges in waterfront hotels? Hedwig has her dancers to look after her; she has the troupe for support. What do I have but a hotel of pensioners with failing lungs?

I stay up late on third floor peering around corners. Certain she isn't in her room, I slide a sheet of paper under her door. In the morning I check to see if it has been moved. There it is. No change.

Wrapped in a wool blanket, I spend a night on three stairs next to her room, stairs leading to a supply closet where Burl keeps his mops and disinfectants. I try to be discreet. This kind of thing has gotten me in trouble when—in guest rooms and in laundry rooms of hotels—I have done unsavory things. The trouble has led me ever northward. From Chicago to Milwaukee; Milwaukee to Oshkosh; Oshkosh to Wausau; Wausau to Rice Lake, when the King Edward Inn was still open; Rice Lake finally here to "the Zenith City of the Unsalted Seas" and fourth foggiest city in the nation. Where do you go after Duluth?

By sitting here, I cannot miss her return. On the tiled steps, I lean against the wall, doze until a pensioner, more dead than alive, stumbles his way to the bathroom. Eventually, the hacking and coughing quiets. Among the old, someone afoot at this hour is no cause for alarm. In rooms up and down the halls of the hotel, sick men clutch wallets and coin purses and suppress their dry coughs per my orders.

Hearing a creak, hearing a taxi hurry away, I look up, wishing for her. I bring another blanket. No one cares what I do. The roomers want to stay out of the fog as I stare at her door. Hedwig's and mine, I like to think: our dresser, our bed, our door, our paradise. All of them ours. Both the door and the frame are painted brown to complement the beige of the walls. The door separates me from her. I stand before it, blankets about my shoulders. Those who rise for the bathroom exchange no pleasantries.

Very late one night I find myself peering in the keyhole. I've forgotten how I'd covered it on the other side when I occupied the room. Seeking privacy, I'd placed black tape over the inside. In the keyhole is nothing but blackness. I bet that on the other side is a room transformed. No doubt she's brought lavender-scented curtains and, from the florist, a bouquet for the nightstand. No doubt she's stuffed the coverlet beneath the bed and replaced it with a counterpane from the department store.

At four a.m., I return to the lobby. Placing my pillow on the supply closet's steps the next night, and with the old blankets around me, I pretend to polish brass fixtures again. I work ten minutes on the fire extinguisher. I feel the doorknob of 301. I run my hands over it. On my knees I lower my head to peek at all the sheets of paper I've been leaving. NO LOVING EVER AGAIN, I add to the set of rules. I recall how once a door had locked on me. The locksmith said it wasn't the lock, strangely, but the mechanism inside the housing causing the problem. Part of it had fallen in such a way as to jam the lock. It wasn't the lock, but the mechanism. With my polishing cloth and a can of Brasso, I rub the plate beneath the doorknob where lies the mechanism that caused a problem. I return to the lobby much later and fall asleep on my cot. Again the rule: NO LOVING ANYONE! NEVER!

Each time I come upstairs now, I think of the mechanism that's buried in the lock's housing, waiting perhaps to trip again. I cannot get the cold secrets of mechanisms out of my head. I imagine them in perfect order; each turn of the doorknob moves the mechanism. I live in a world that keys lock and release. I dream of open doors. I see all secret mechanisms. They are in working order—well-oiled perfection. But other times bolts spring shut. I am uncomfortable in this mysterious world. I return to gaze into the keyhole or to speculate on the secrets of the mechanism in the door lock, the mechanism of exclusion, darkness. It is as if her door alone comes to symbolize the times I've been separated from others and have tried to peek at them.

I recall as a child my stepmother's door being closed to me when my father went into the bedroom on Saturday afternoons. I recall a church door shut against me. Jesus did not do this. It was the sinners He died for doing it. I saw the choir loft lit up, singers practicing, but the mechanism in the door had slipped shut on me when I had every right to be inside where my stepmother had sent me to teach me not to peek. The best I could do that time was hum along outside. I began to sing as it grew colder, until finally I was hollering against the night and the singing. I'd been shut out again, this time from a downtown movie house where I'd gone to dream away an afternoon. Pulling on the door, I'd found it shut fast. I looked up. FOR SALE read the marquee. The empty place was just beyond reach, the incredible, deep privacy of an old movie house that once showed X-rated movies.

Doors end openness, curtail your freedom. You can't enter when a door is shut on you. You aren't supposed to. Something always has to end during such an exchange. Someone loses. I have had trouble and now have come northward. I imagine all of the Chopin's doors thrown wide so I can choose into which rooms to go. What are keyholes that they should keep me lonely? What is the darkness? Why must I peek from the outside?

On the afternoon of Hedwig's last day at the hotel, my sanity returns. I am alone in the Hotel Chopin with the springs and bolts of its doors. The hotel has been my private pleasure. I go now for the wicker basket, place bread and wine in it. I tuck four or five bouquets of plastic flowers in it from the lobby. I crank all of it to the landing. Arms full, I cannot help myself. Before I know it, I am past the threshold, stealing into her third floor room. How different it might have been had Hedwig, opening it, said, "Come in, Harold." But she hasn't been here in a month.

If it is brighter in the hallway, the place lit by rose-shaded bulbs, inside her room it is dark, the shade drawn. On the dresser lies a hairbrush, a bottle of shampoo, a face towel. The bed isn't made. The old coverlet is thrown back, sheets mussed. I have wanted to live in a simpler time without doors like that on Hedwig's room. In this earlier time, I'd rest outside in a bed of flowers, drink my wine, eat the bread, and call to the maiden folk dancers in the forest night, but this is not at all as I expected. Dust has accumulated on the windowsill. The paint on the radiator flakes in large pieces, some of which fall like broken hearts to the floor.

I tuck in the white sheet and smooth the coverlet. With my pocket comb, I pull hair from her brush. Most of it I throw in the wastebasket. Some I save for myself, the petty thief. The face towel I fold and place beside the brush. I straighten a photo in the mirror. I place flowers around. One obligation remains. I turn to the door that does not fit. At the top it slants a half-inch downward. Holding the edge of the waste basket to the knob of the uppermost pin, I force the pin up and out. The other upper hinge pin I pull out as well. With the lower two, I do the same, then lift the door—number 301—from its hinges, propping it in the hallway. This done I sit on the love seat, legs over the side. I open the wine, cut off a piece of bread and cheese. Eating, drinking, I stay here for an hour. When I rise slowly to welcome evening and remove more doors from hinge and frame, the first dancers are returning from their performance.

"Where's the wicker basket?" they are calling from the second floor. "Harry, where are you and your basket?"

I hear voices on the landing, hear them over the coughing of the tenants. The dancers are nearing. They stand outside looking at the door I have removed to allow free passage to Hedwig Wesolewski's room. All the third floor rooms are doorless.

"Come in," I call to them from the love seat. They are pointing at me, giggling. Disgusted, some of them turn and leave.

"Don't go. Help me finish the wine. Then we'll open all the rooms like this one and have a dance party."

Others come to laugh. I hear someone saying the police and the Zgoda manager had best be notified, then Hedwig, whose room it is. But through it all, through all the insults and giggles, I, Harold Hansen, hotelier, sit privately with wine and bread in the love seat in the meadow of plastic flowers.

Great Sea Battles

If you go down to Hog Island on the Superior waterfront, you will see where my uncle Louie fought a great sea battle. Like most men, he was reluctant to go to war. Being fourteen-years-old, I'd never fought in war, but this changed during the month I will tell you about. Whereas Louie was already battle-scarred from marriage, you could say I was in an intelligence unit behind the lines and therefore never faced the direct fire he did, although I suffered wounds.

When the big war started, he asked Rae-Rita, the southern lady he married, to reconsider the ultimatum she'd given him. He called her "Honey Babe." When she said, "No, that's final!", he set a foot reluctantly into his boat. Its bow rested on bottom muck and weeds, aft end floating free. As he brought in the other foot, the boat, a fourteen-footer with a fifteen-horsepower outboard, rocked softly from side to side. "Please don't send me to sea after ten years in the real navy. I hate the water," he said. He had the outboard tilted up. He crouched low on the way back to it.

Everything his wife, my aunt, said to him was an order. Never could she ask in a polite way, "Louie, please raise the faded flag of your surrender." No, she commanded him, "Pull up the flag!" Hands on her hips, the fleet admiral snapped her bubble gum. Then my mother, the vice admiral, started. "Show us how you've reformed, Louie. Show us the flag of your sincere regret."

He swore under his breath. With rope, he'd tied an eight-foot willow branch to the outboard. From its end hung a dingy white pillowcase. Dangling half in the water, it looked like the flag of a defeated man until he swore again.

"Go on, raise the flag," Rae-Rita said.

Saluting her, he grabbed the willow branch to do as she said. It ruffled a moment in the warm land breeze, then gave up and hung down. Seeing my uncle robbed of his manhood, I left the three of them. Walking across the railroad tracks and up through the field, I watched Louie shove off with a paddle, Ma and Rae-Rita waving to him. Though I believe she might have been crying, it wasn't long before she got after *me* with orders.

"Allen, pull up your trousers. I'm tired of seeing them dragging all day," she said. "I'll miss your uncle."

"Allen," Ma said, "see that you get your hair cut. And please don't come home without it short enough, or I'll take the scissors to it."

"Yes," I said.

We all looked back at Louie on Superior Bay. Actually, it is an inlet he was on. What we call the big bay stands on the other side of Hog Island. Then comes the Minnesota Point sandbar. Then Lake Superior. He was sailing the shallows between Hog Island and the mainland. His boat left a "v" in its wake.

When we got home, I stayed outside to avoid Rae-Rita's orders. With the two of them eating candy on the sofa, I was pretty safe. When *As the World Turns* ended, however, I had to listen up for their orders. I sat in a lawn chair beneath the window. Through the screen, I could hear them discuss my uncle. "Too much video poker, too much gambling. That's the problem. Now he's between jobs again," they said.

"With his addictive personality, it's a good thing he never took to drinking. He'd be hooked on one more habit," Ma said. "Give me another of those cream-filled candies, will you? I like peanut-filled as well. Which are your favorites, Rae-honey? Le Bon Bons?"

"I like cream-filled."

"Oh, my mistake," Ma said. "You take this one then."

"No, you have it."

"But, honey, I have to watch my figure," Ma said. "Both of us do. You not so much. You're younger, which is an advantage. You've got to stay shapely for his return from—what does he call it?"

"His Voyage of Penance," I said through the window screen.

"Voyage of Penance. You've got to keep your figure, Rae."

"He has the kind of personality," Rae-Rita said, "that it can't control itself. If he likes something, there's no stopping him, but he has to have it. He was that way with me *and* video poker. He lacks self control. Hand me another chocolate. I'll try the peanut-filled. No, a caramel cluster. Then let's open the Brach's box to see what that candy company offers two lonely ladies."

"I have a catalog from the store that opened in the Mariner Mall," Ma said. "Called 'The Ample Lady,' the place is for bigger gals like us to buy clothes at."

"It's next to the candy shop," Rae-Rita said.

"How did you know?" I asked.

"About Louie's lack of self control," Rae-Rita went on as if she didn't hear me, "this is the best way to break him of a bad habit. Get him out on the bay away from temptation. Make it a Voyage of Repentance and Penance. We can't afford fancy rest cures like movie stars get. As long as he stays temptation-free out there, this isn't going to cost us and it might cure him. What were you saying about ample ladies? Were you calling me ample? Fat is a feminist issue, although we do both wear plus sizes."

"I meant nothing, Rae-Rita. You are my feminist sister. Boy!" Ma called.

"Right here, Ma and Rae-Rita."

"Seeing you're now the man around here, get your mother and me the Ding Dongs."

"Honey, bring us crackers and cheese before that."

After giving me an order, they'd forget me while I carried it out.

"I was saying it's his lack of self control that causes Louie such trouble. He don't understand feminist anger neither."

"But Rae-Rita, honey, if there's anyone to straighten him out, it's you. Who do you think he's sitting out there by himself dreaming about? Here's a man who will sit in a fourteen-foot Alumacraft for as long as it takes to break himself of a habit. 'Get thee behind me, Satan! Take your temptations away!' Now I'd say that's a compliment to you."

My aunt Rae-Rita wore pink lipstick you had to wash from the glass after she took a drink of something. When she was dolling up, she kept her forehead curls in place with strips of cellophane tape. Embarrassed by Ma's compliment, she fiddled with the tape when I brought their order from the kitchen. "Your crackers and Ding Dongs," I said. But Ma complained, "You know I like the low-fat crackers. Get them."

"That doesn't make sense. You've got high-fat chocolate Ding Dongs," I said. Uncle Louie would point out such things about Ma and Rae-Rita's thinking. A small man against two large women hasn't got a chance, though. He didn't weigh 170 pounds, I bet, which put him thirty pounds less than Rae-Rita, forty less than Ma. I have seen Rae-Rita sit on him.

As the day wore on, I expected my uncle would return at any time. He'd approach the shore, his outboard a low purr against the croaking frogs. "I am here to conquer sin," he'd announce, and I'd be happy he was back. Each day he had an hour to clean up and change clothes before Rae-Rita said, "You have a gambler's misery," and point her hand toward the boat.

"What you've earned at work you always lost," Ma'd cry.

So maybe it *was* good he was out there in his boat on the inlet if it kept him away from video poker, which you can play in bars and at Indian casinos. I grew to like the idea of his fighting sin. The bay was the best place to wring your hands and weep for salvation.

"Louie has to lose himself to find himself," Ma'd say. "When there is no more poker playing, salvation has its chance to work."

At night through my window, I'd hear crying and hollering—such noises down on the bay as you could never imagine. This was the anguish of a man going through hell on earth.

My uncle had a tent aboard. He'd put it up at night or when it rained. For three weeks, he stayed out rocking on the waters, and I thought it was all for Rae-Rita. Then one morning when he edged up to a stump and propped his paddle in the muck, I began to suspect his method of penance.

"Did you sleep okay last night? You look worn out. You'll be coming in soon, won't you?" I asked.

"There are things to figure out. If you need me, I'm always close in here around the swamp or bay with my lines strung watching the stars." He tossed me the fish he'd caught. "Can you keep a secret?" He scratched his cheek where a mosquito must have bitten him.

"Sure," I said.

"Journey of Penance," he muttered.

"Is that water you're drinking? I can get you some that's fresh."

"This ain't water," he said. He looked a mess, weary and happy at the same time. His brown hair was tangled. His eyes had a hard time adjusting to the morning light. He was holding a bottle. I didn't know whether I'd dreamt it or not, but I thought I remembered music last night and voices talking down here.

Taking another sip, he closed the bottle. Then he got red-faced—seasick, I figured, from sitting in the boat, from the morning's heat, or from what he'd just drank. He lost the look of Grace Abounding Ma says you get when you're pure of heart. Grabbing the paddle, he pushed his boat out, started the motor, and headed for deeper water. He has reasons for sailing early, I told myself. I'd bring his lunch later.

I saw him off and went home confused about his behavior, so

that it was going on twenty-eight days. Between snapping her gum, Rae-Rita kept saying, "He'll cure himself. I bet he never looks at another video poker machine or playing card. He's doing it for me I am happy to say."

"Now remember, Rae-Rita, he's still a sick man out there," Ma would say.

"You aren't kidding. Twenty-eight days, by gosh. He must love me!"

Because I was their servant, they started in again. "Allen, get the assorted lunchmeats for your Ma so she can eat a lunch and watch her shows. She's had a terrible morning. I got a laundry load to do. Can you possibly see about it if you've got time? Be a dear."

Then on the thirtieth day of Uncle Louie's great sea battle, Ma got a brainstorm. Possibly it came after I told her how happy he looked. Possibly it was the way the sun slanted off the porch roof. Maybe the sun gave her heatstroke and changed her way of thinking. She got the idea that perhaps Uncle Louie wanted to be out there, that no matter what we did he wouldn't come back from the sea. Pulling off her glasses, she said, "Rae-Rita, thirty days is enough to find spiritual peace in the Lord. It took Jesus forty days and nights. But Louie is only a mortal."

In a minute, we were out the door, down the path, and across the tracks. We didn't see him out there. Ma pointed her fists and screwed up her face trying to figure where he could be. After a long wait, I saw him come from the swamp far away. He didn't appear to notice when Ma and Rae-Rita commenced hollering and threatening. It was getting toward evening. We built a driftwood fire. When the mosquitoes forced us to retreat, Ma and Rae-Rita talked themselves into opening a box of Fanny Farmer chocolates, which made it easier for them to forget my uncle.

It went on like this, Louie oblivious to our efforts, until the end of the week. Ma and Rae-Rita were fuming. Word had gotten around that he refused to come off of the bay. Other women came over.

"My husband's been acting strange, too," said Mrs. Bates.

"And mine," said Mrs. Rehnstrand.

"You know how they idolize Louie," Mrs. Popovich said. "They follow him around. The fellows can't seem to do without him."

I sat outside in the yard gathering sensitive intelligence for Louie about the troop movements of women.

"I'll be darned," Ma said.

Then Mrs. Purcell piped in. "You give them alcohol and some of them will desert a woman and her children."

Ma and Rae-Rita were really steamed by now. Ma called Aunt Birdie on the phone. I could hear her shouting, "He's traded one sin in for another, Bird, and now I can't believe he's planning to come in off that boat. Call Hattie," Ma said.

Birdie called Hattie, her sister, who lives in the next block over. Hattie called Mrs. Maybelline; Mrs. Maybelline called Mrs. Culver; Mrs. Culver called Miss Ritterbusch—until all the girls and relations knew that Louie wasn't coming back soon.

The first thing next morning when it got light, we were down there—Rae-Rita, me, Ma, Hattie, Birdie—confronting him. When he saw us, he was cruising downshore past the swamp by an old willow that'd fallen into the bay.

He angled toward shore, all along, sneaky-like, eyeing us up, for when Rae-Rita, Ma, and the others started hollering, just as slow as you please he made a wide circle I'd seen him practicing out there, and grinning, shook his hat and headed for deeper water. Hooting, cussing, turning the boat for all she was worth, he appeared like a giant in the Sears and Roebuck Variable Powered Telescope I brought along. He put his hands to his nose. Wiggling his fingers, he made a gesture at Rae-Rita and Ma.

"You're a spiteful creature, Louie, but don't for a moment think the Lord above is not watching! You won't go boating on the Lake of Fire," Ma yelled. "There are no U-turns on the road to hell!" She rolled up her pantslegs. In her frenzy, she waded out through mud, sticks, and weeds.

Still he went round and round, veering in, scaring Ma as he

did, then shooting out further than before, all the while tilting some contaminated drinking water to his mouth, smiling, and waving the crazy white flag in defiance of them. It was the same flag as before only proud now in a strong sailor's hands. Then I began contemplating a life at sea. In front of everybody, all of them, admiral, vice admiral, everyone, I imagined myself in uniform, hat tipped forward. It was Louie's flag and the boat I liked so much. In the telescope, I could see them plainly until Rae-Rita took it away and folded it up.

"You've got no business being with respectable people," she said. She pulled me off to the side. "You're with us or against us, for we're all respectable women. Choose sides ... your Ma and me, or that—" She pointed to where Louie was rocking the boat—"that drunken sailor!"

"Hey," he yelled and held up the bottle. "Anchors Aweigh!" His voice came clearly to me over the water. I felt the pull of the sea the way men have since the start of time. When Rae-Rita made a grab for me, I pushed loose. Kicking off my shirt and tennis shoes, I made it through the pack of them and into the water. Going out, I passed Ma. Her clothes soaked, water dripping from her hair, she was wading in. Some weeds hung off her one ear, the starboard ear. As I glided past, knifing through the water, she glared at me, tried to say something, but murky water came out of her mouth. Unaccustomed to the ways of the sea, she sputtered and gave up.

Then it was just me, an able-bodied seaman, still laughing, heading out toward the cool depths and safety of Uncle Louie's boat. Halfway out, I could hear him piping me aboard.

The Woman Who Ate Cat Food

A telephone solicitor who worked out of her apartment, Margaret Markham loved the feel of the receiver against her cheek, loved greeting potential customers—her voice caressing a man's ear with offers of a week in Cancun, a sweat-free toilet, a transmission flush with his tune-up. This was before DO NOT CALL lists, cell phones, and mass telemarketing. So appealing was her voice that, as she spoke, men dreamt of the color of her eyes and hair. They loved her voice as much as women loved Luther Craft's voice on KSAD radio or, later, on his *Night Train* radio show at 1390 AM. That voice, Margaret's, offered possibilities if you answered your telephone.

A month before she went to hell, the woman who lived for dial tones made a sale that led to a social encounter that blossomed into a romance. Solicitor and solicited met for dinner using the "Carriage Trade Plan" she'd sold him over the phone. For a $20.50 investment, the plan entitles a person to purchase a meal and receive another free at various Twin Ports restaurants. The man she made the sale to used his card so often with her that soon the hand-breaded chicken dinners at Eddie's in Superior, the lasagna dinners at The Gopher in West Duluth, and the pizzas at Sammy's Pizza in both cities began to show around his waist. A picky eater, his date stayed at 110 pounds.

"Margaret," he said the last Wednesday of their friendship. He'd come with ashes on his forehead. "Margaret, the children, Greta, and I...we're leaving. Business has called me away, dear. We're moving to Fargo-Moorhead."

After hearty meals at the Hammond Steak House, Pickwick, Black Steer, and Dreamland Supper Club, he'd gained forty pounds. He was no longer the firm, fit man Margaret had encountered on the telephone a month before. She watched him leave for good one rainy Saturday. From a café window, she saw the difficult time he had getting into his car. The month of passionate suppers had blown him up so that he could have used a fast during Lent when the devout deny themselves pleasures. A fast would have gone well with the ashes on his forehead that Ash Wednesday. From a phone booth in West Duluth, Margaret Markham scribbled down numbers off of the wall. Since any number would do, she called 394-8471, a Superior number, and struck up a conversation with a Bob Harnitz, who quickly lodged a complaint with Wisconsin Bell when she insisted on meeting him, a stranger, within the hour. "Intentional annoyance by use of the phone... The maximum penalty for violation is—" the phone company warned her.

After this, except for telephone contacts made from her room, it was as if she no longer existed. For all anyone in the apartment building knew, she'd moved to the seedy Hotel Chopin in Duluth or, worse, to the Heartbreak Hotel in Superior. Without hope, she sat alone in the dim, cold apartment thinking about telephone talks she could have with the man next door. If he'd only call her and say something kind, it would mean the way out of failure and despair through friendship. Needing a gentle voice after the breakup with the married man who'd gained weight, she waited for a call. She grew weak waiting for the call from Apartment 24, from anyone in the building, from anyone in the Twin Ports really. If she did go out, she took the back way. For a time you'd think she was on an out-of-town trip, a holiday. Then the man next door in Apartment 24 would spot her locking her door, hurrying Lord knows where—perhaps to a phone booth to copy down numbers or to leave her number. She was preoccupied with phones, compulsive about the numbers that enable you to contact others in a lonely world, strangers even.

The man next door, a writer of obscure short stories, would say someone has taken poetic license with him. "I didn't deny her the comfort of my wonderful mind as often as you'd think, but I confess I needed to know things about her." In his defense he says this to Laura and Fred, relatives of the phone solicitor, who've flown in for the funeral. By now what he says doesn't matter. As Laura and Fred were coming from Houston, Margaret herself was on her way somewhere else after what had suddenly become, on Ash Wednesday, a not-so-happy life telephoning others about (Laura would say it this way) "siding on their houses, warranties on their appliances, insurance on their lov—, on their lives. Look, I almost said loves a minute ago, Fred. I almost said 'insurance on their loves.' Love insurance. Is there such a thing?"

"That's pretty funny how the mind tricks us," Fred says.

They are standing in the hallway outside Margaret's apartment, making the acquaintance of the story writer. Fred has barely unpacked his bags at the hotel and taken a look around Superior, Wisconsin, before coming over where Laura has been a few hours. He strokes the cat, Cupcake, who has returned from chasing Margaret Markham's soul through the city's streets and alleys. The police who discovered Margaret Markham said that when they opened the window of her apartment, the cat leapt out, landing on its paws, and took off down Tower Avenue after her spirit. Now he'd come home.

"Without this little rascal to keep her sane," Fred says, holding the cat in his arms, "she might have gotten a black touch-tone telephone to show how depressed she was, instead of the dial-type phone she had, or she might have had the phone disconnected entirely."

"So instead she disconnected herself," says Laura, trying not to cry again. "To think my sister—"

"I know one thing," says the man next door who is also a part-time instructor at the small college in Superior. "It was hard getting hold of her. I bumped into her once, one of those days she'd gone out. By the way, may I call you Fred and Laura?"

More comfortable with each other and despite Laura's grief, they grow cheerful for a few minutes, the men.

"Please," says Fred. "Why all the formality in the first place?"

"As I said, I bumped into her once," the man next door says. "She was winded from climbing those stairs. I looked in on her, found her making phone calls. '3409 is busy,' she'd say and look at me. '7041, Hello? Mr. Hagadorn?' She'd turn and say, 'He hung up!' Then she'd dial again. '5445? Mr. Schuster?' She was totally committed to telephone soliciting. She loved telephones."

"That was my sister," Laura replies.

"One time I found her eating Cupcake's food. You know, the only incoming calls she got were from teenagers, cranks. 'Do you have Prince Albert in the can? Is Jack Mehoff there?' they'd ask. 'May I please speak with Master Bates?' She'd hear laughing. Then...click, the line goes dead. They'd hang up. She'd be alone giggling. One night she told me this and a lot of other things I'd asked her about."

"Maybe that's when she thought of having it disconnected," Fred says, "when she got the crank calls."

"I don't know. Maybe. She found out who *I* was from my mailbox. You might've seen the name down there. Randy Pepper."

"You say you teach in a college. Doesn't that make you Dr. Pepper?"

"I have a Master of Arts. I'm working on my Ph.D. By the way, it's no ordinary college where I teach part-time. It's 'Wisconsin's Leading Public Liberal Arts College.'"

Unimpressed, Fred says, "This is a good cat. You wonder what it's witnessed."

"Yes, you wonder," Mr. Pepper says. "All I know is she'd make plenty of phone calls, then, exhausted, she'd spoon out her anxieties with Cupcake's Moist Meals and Junior Friskies. 'What are we having tonight?' she'd ask Cupcake. She had secrets galore."

"She was always that way," Laura says.

"She padded her shoes with paper towels when her shoes got too big for her," says the neighbor. "That's one thing she told me. Do you remember when she was nineteen, Laura? When she lost her first boyfriend? One night he had to go in early, she told me. No sooner had she left him than two girls came by to get him. She told me she stood out of sight hugging the rotting barn, watching for him the time her boyfriend did that to her."

"I remember," says Laura. "She came home laughing when she should have been crying. 'Ma,' she said, 'I saw two girls just now at Arthur's house, which means his mother knew he was going out on me, so I was doubly deceived.'"

"Isn't it kind of cold for April?" asks Fred.

"A week ago it was warm," the neighbor says. "Now it's freezing."

"At the age of forty-three with her hair the color of ash she must have waited for us to call her," Laura is saying. "How lonely Margaret always was. My sister tended to colors like dust and ash, the brown of dead leaves on gray trees. She knew how to celebrate Lent."

"I'd say so," says the neighbor, "a very passionate celebrant. For her there was no resurrection, just fast and abstain day after day. 'Hello,' she'd say. 'Mr. Mitchell, 399-8652? It's Margaret Markham for Superior Aluminum. Our name says it all. I wonder if we could talk about your siding, which our representative noticed—'"

"'Thanks, no,' he'd tell her.

"'Mr. Reginald Fortier? I've called to see if we could talk life insurance—'

"'No, thanks.'"

"I guess that's what her life amounted to," says Fred, "the empty, white page of rejection to go along with the black touch-tone she always wanted. She was a blank."

"Then she met you," Laura says. "What did you do to her?"

"Nothing. I came in once after rapping on the door and getting no answer. I found her sitting with an empty glass to her ear. She was holding it against the wall, trying to hear me in my apartment. She'd been listening to the wall for maybe three hours. When she saw me, she looked up and said, 'Do you know what you find when you dial yourself on the telephone?—that on the other end, you yourself are busy.' That's all! That's what she said. All your sister had in the final analysis was a busy signal telling her her line was engaged. All she had was the outside world by telephone and my capricious humor next door. Heh, heh," he chuckles to himself, forgiving his shortcomings which are modest ones, he believes.

"What I can't figure out," says Fred, "is how anyone could be that lonely. Now take Laura and me, sure we get lonesome, but not so bad that we'd— Why was she caught here like this? I guess she was just weary of people not talking or being rude or filing complaints with the phone company. This all seems ridiculous now."

"It's a little late to be much help. Except maybe to you, Laura," says Mr. Pepper.

"Thank you. I appreciate your sympathy. She had a confused life. I never expected it was this bad."

The neighbor looks up and down the hall. It is bleak, quiet. The three of them huddle under the light.

"She was interesting for me to write about. Maybe I shouldn't tell you, but I was in her place on one of the last nights when she made calls for I think it was East End Awnings. A guy named Kruks answered. I guess he wept, then swore at her. Do you know what she said? 'Mr. Kruks, talk to me, please. I want to hear you. No, don't hang up tonight. It's too close to my day of departure.' This guy Kruks told her his wife Myrna was in a rest home and his son Jerry in the Navy in the Persian Gulf. He must have been off his rocker. He started yelling over the telephone. I could even hear him from where I stood. 'Railroad has laid me off. Thirty-nine years I go night and day. What do I need your awnings for? Damn them to hell. All awnings! Goddamn all of them to everlasting hell. So why do I deserve this? The Church can go to hell … and goddamned hell.

Ralph, my brother, he's got bone cancer. You tell me it's fair now.'"

"This is what I think," Laura says. "She'd just been alone too long to live with it and couldn't go on. She loved all these people she solicited with calls. In her strange way, she loved the suffering, guys like Mr. Kruks. Maybe even you," she says to the neighbor. "But she'd gone this way too long. She probably didn't know how she spent her time anymore. If I know my sister, she probably talked to herself, held the phone in one hand and talked to herself in the mirror."

"She was the sole companion of the self," the neighbor adds.

"She was a human being who was never loved much but wanted to love, and you tell me now she even succeeded in eating cat food. Cheated, she went away. My poor sister Margaret."

"She'd put down the telephone for the last time," Fred says. "The busy signal was in her ears. It was getting serious. Yes, that's what happened."

"Why didn't we help her and come to visit, Fred? Why didn't we make her more than a footnote in life? She must have felt helpless holding the telephone receiver as though it were a ... gun, a clock, a portable radio and she was here waiting for the weather forecast."

"I bet she put Cupcake in the closet. Did she do that, Cupcake, did she?" Fred asks. "Then she closed the door. She must have written the letters at her kitchen table. Putting them in envelopes, she'd leave them in the mailbox for the postman."

"Which meant she went downstairs that last time to mail the letters we got," Mr. Pepper says.

"Yes," says Fred, "that's how we all got the news, from her letters. Then she probably looked in on the cat, maybe freshened its water before returning to her place by the stove where she could sit reviewing her phone bills. What do you think? Was that how it was?"

"I just know what the police and fire people said, that the cat jumped out when they opened the closet door and bedroom window," replies the neighbor.

"We know this much," Laura says. "The cat chased her spirit."

"Where have you been, Cupcake?" asks the neighbor. "Which

way did Margaret go, up or down?"

"Do you suppose she's in heaven? It's too horrible to think otherwise," says Laura.

"Did I tell you I'm writing a story? I've come to see through all this that no one should neglect suffering. I've found that much out, and I am genuinely sorry about your sister." The man next door takes Laura's hand, shakes it. "It's tragic," he says. "The day of her death she mailed something to me. It came in a white envelope with the smell of stove gas clinging to it. The enigma of your sister Margaret. She hardly wrote anything. It arrived two days later the best I can figure it. It took two whole days to go what? Five feet from her place to mine via the postal service. Isn't it amazing what the post office gets away with? All she had to do was walk over and open the door, thus saving stamps. But here comes a letter instead. In the middle of a legal-sized sheet, she wrote five lousy words, 'I, suffering, am done for.' Why did she mail them? Why didn't she knock and come in or slip the letter under my door and save postage? We'll never know, Fred and Laura."

"We won't, that's for sure," says Fred.

"Gee, we've been out here a long time," Laura says, beginning to cry again.

The neighbor looks at his watch.

"Fred, Laura," he says, "look, it was my pleasure meeting you two and again, my condolences. I've got to get back to work. I'll excuse myself. I'm writing the story for publication."

"Good luck with it," Fred says. Together, he and Laura fumble with the lock to Margaret Markham's apartment, Number 23.

Once inside, the man next door realizes he has taken a chill. The hall was drafty. He hears the traffic on Tower, then Fred and Laura next door. He hears a thump as though they're moving furniture. He hears them talking. Sitting down at the kitchen table, he looks out over the street and writes in pencil on a legal-sized pad:

I had pushed her on by giving her the forecast she wanted. She'd made up her mind to believe anything I said. I'd been thinking about her a few days and how I'd use her in a short story I planned. Then I ended up using her! Calling her, I said, half in jest, "Your story is over." She sighed, hung up. Now that her story is done, how shall I end my story? Others she solicited are partly responsible for her fate, but I am mainly the one—

Mr. Pepper, the writer, hears Fred and Laura raising their voices. Putting down the pencil, he reads what he has written, tears it up, throws it in the waste basket by his chair. With an empty glass to his ear, he proceeds to the wall. He can just make out Fred's talking, but the words are indistinct. It's just Fred from Houston, Texas, talking.

I am waiting for a phone call from Margaret, he thinks. He checks to make sure the receiver is off the hook, even dials himself. I am in a perfect hell of my own waiting for a telephone message from the sister and sister-in-law of the couple next door who are talking in the kitchen near the gas stove. If I keep the phone tied up and off the hook, she won't get through to me. Not at first. Eventually she will, though, thinks Mr. Pepper. I'll let it ring a few dozen times, hoping it's a crank asking for Jack Mehoff. When the time comes, it won't be a crank call. I'll pick up the receiver as I now do in practice and hear the patient voice, "Hello, I have a collect call from Miss or Mrs. Margaret Markham. Will you accept the charges?" I'll agree to pay for the call, but when the operator hangs up, I'll be left with nothing but the silences of years and miles, deathly silences that finally decide to renew acquaintances.

Ice Days

In the northern woods far from God's light, Paul, a sinner, stood at the edge of a clearing. A rope held the sack about his neck. "Over here, Gunnar," he said. "How's your mother?"

"She complains of the cold," Gunnar said. "But I have no complaints. How would my getting cold look to the rest of you?"

"If I were you, I wouldn't admit it either. You are a missionary," said Paul as Gunnar hurried past him through the thicket into the wind. Gunnar thought, *The cold has taken him. Paul wanders the cold frozen with sin. He's far from the sun in this northern outpost.*

Guiding himself by the cross on its roof, Gunnar headed toward the home he'd built to face the cardinal points so he couldn't stray.

Wandering, I'm not lost, not with the cross to guide me. One can pray and mend one's ways. The owls, wolves, and bobcats are lost. Paul with the sack about his neck, the others, the hundreds of others, they are treacherous, evil, mean-spirited sinners consumed. But me? No.

In the failing light, he made it home. The wooden cross looked somber against the sky. There were paths to the strange places where dead spirits waited. At night the air filled with the smoke of the fires that didn't warm them. *The stinging night offers them nothing,* thought Gunnar. *There is little consolation in the eternal winter of this cold, dark place, only the snow drifting about the shelter's eaves on St. Lucia's night to protect them from the wind.*

Despite the paths available to him, Gunnar broke a new path to avoid the cardinal points. The cardinal points were good points from which lost, wandering souls could learn—as they could from the crucifix. But you sometimes couldn't see East, West, South, or North in the night, and sometimes the cross was merely a shadow. He had done right, Gunnar told himself, to make a new path and to save for sinners the ones that approached from the cardinal points. That was the right thing to do.

"Gunnar!" she hollered and struck the tin kettle with her hammer. She expects something, thought Gunnar. *A storm? Her death? Is that what she's doing? Banging a storm and death away with an alarm kettle? Keeping her own death at arm's length? Is she outbanging the noise of her sins with that hammer, outfoxing the noise of the cold with those blankets, those walls? I am doing right building her inward, for strong walls can keep sin out. The strong walls of determination keep Syl Magda safe inside. My mother. Mine. Syl Magda. No sin, shame, strife shall enter here tonight. Nothing shall attach itself here.*

She lay in bed complaining when he came in from the snow that had begun falling. When he told her, "the ice sparkles when the moon comes out. Will you look at it with me?," she banged out her answer on the hammer and kettle. When he said to her, "Mama, I'm going out shooting if the full moon appears again," she wouldn't listen but kept banging at the kettle. "Father in heaven," Gunnar prayed. Outside, the fox made off with the chickens. It was a sad, strange thing all around.

"Do you hear it in the chimney?" she asked.

"No."

In the house he'd put on a lighter coat. He'd succeeded in boarding up an inside window—not with the broken hammer he'd fixed and given back to her to bang the kettle, but with the good, sturdy hammer.

"Try to sleep," he said.

"No, put more rags under the door. I'm cold," she said.

"More rags," said Gunnar.

Clutching the hammer, he went to work on the other side of the room, where the fresh-hewn boards stood. With the saw, nails, chisel, plane, the rule, the two hammers, one sturdy, one broken, he worked on the north wall. He was building walls to shut Syl Magda in and keep her from cold. Outside, the world's sins and the cold wind, but inside the walls would keep her safe, warm, and quiet.

The pattern of the inner walls followed those of the outer walls. Already he'd raised beams and made a roof four feet below the original. The walls of the cabin: they were 30 X 35, the next room's 20 X 25. To keep her from evil, he'd built a house within a house, a cabin within a cabin, a prayer shelter within a prayer shelter. Then there was the newest room. Third, innermost, it stood another few feet in from the last one he'd built. He was working on it now.

Outside all these walls, the wind shook the treetops. In the new room, he caulked whatever holes or knots appeared in the boards. He had built the room within the room with windows so you could look right out through three prayer shelters—one inside (or outside) the next—to trees, to firs and white birches, trees of night and winter time. But now he was boarding up these windows, not building or refurbishing the shelter and the windows, but boarding them up.

"Under the door there's a draft."

"Under which door?"

"I don't know. I'm mixed up," she said.

"There's nowhere else to move you. I'll cover you with my heavy coat."

He blew sawdust away from where he was working, lay the coat gently on the four-post bed, which was handmade like everything here. Inside in the center she lay, her bed raised on wooden blocks. On the elevated bed, she came up to his chest.

"The chimney, is he there?"

"No," said Gunnar.

The woodstove by her bed provided heat to the cabin. Dust and soot filtered down when he craned his neck up into the cold fireplace chimney. (There were three fireplaces in the cabin, too. He had laid stones for all of them. In every way, the three fireplaces were identical.) He was busying himself inside the shelter now.

She was right. In the chimney darkness: there was something up there.

He opened the door, rushed the few feet to the next door, and through that to the next. Outside it was a night where sin lived. He shielded his eyes against the moon, saw something above. Now the river heaved and dislodged its ice in patterns on the shore.

"Come down!" he called.

He could barely hear his mother saying, "Do you hear it in the chimney outside?"

He didn't answer. He could hear her hammering a warning to the night.

The wind swirled. He raced back to the door. The wind ripped at his coat. Sweeping the snow away, he slammed the big door shut, slammed another.

"Stay in," she said as he slammed the third door shut. "Don't go. This night help to keep me from trouble. I'm seventy-nine."

She's not seventy-nine. She's little more than fifty-four. He didn't know what made her talk so. He thought of leaving forever the innermost shelter with the raised bed in the center. There was too much to find out in the forest. Sometimes he watched the night wheel by. Dressed in furs down on the river, he thought how he'd never been part of the night world, not like the beasts whose skins he wore. In this cold land west of Two Heart, he'd observed night and sin but neither embraced nor understood them. Sin and the night world—he'd never understood them.

He and Syl Magda, his mother, had traveled here long ago searching for Gunnar's father, who'd set out from Värmland in Sweden. He'd sailed N-NW, becoming trapped in the ice, at which time he'd stepped out upon the high places and mountains and windrows. In the white wasteland, he did not die spiritually. No spiritual wanderer, he was a good, honest believer. The peasants who found him brought him to the nearest village, named *Paradis* of all things—or *Djurgaard*. Finding Gunnar's father on the northern ice, they'd sent him to *Paradis* and continued their own journeys looking, in sorrowful penitence, for loved ones who themselves had died, though in less desirable ways.

Gunnar had now spent twenty-two years in the Lord's service in America. Did one never quit serving God? He'd never had a reason to fear for his soul. "You can't and won't sin," they'd told him in the church as a child in Värmland. Over the years he'd prayed and kept the lights in the prayer shelter's windows on, lights in the night of death and sorrow. It was his mission. *I'm ministering to dead souls in this outpost of faith. I can teach them. Like Paul, the owl man, they are doomed, but I can teach them why they wander.* He kept a light in the prayer shelter so that if they should look in, it would be on the workings of a prayerful family, the mother and son, Gunnar and Syl Magda Johannsen. *As the farmer reaps wheat, so must I, at such great distance from the sun, reap snow.*

"The chimney!" she said.

From the roof, he heard cries. He didn't believe there was anyone out there. He stoked wood, added a log, went to bed. A believer, he was no part of this night world. He'd sinned only in the smallest ways. He'd felt neither terrible cold like her nor the night of sin. "There's no man up there," he yelled. "Nothing. No one."

Because he slept just outside the newest room (third, innermost), he found he must wear skins and furs to ward off the cold.

In the morning he sprang up, went outside to check the prayer shelter. He hurried back in, shut the door, then the next. It was a bad morning. It chilled him. Not with the chill of sin, of course. Was his mother possessed of the night and cold? he wondered, closing the last door.

She held out her hands.

He soothed her. "What is he like, Gunnar Johannsen?" she whispered.

"No one is out there, no thing, Mama," he said.

"Well, do you have to keep going out?" she asked.

"I can work inside on your room. Are you any warmer? It's bad out, terribly cold today."

"No warmer. Is he up there?"

"No one is up there, no," Gunnar said.

"You're lying. He's coming down trying to get me. I think he's the cold heart of my nature."

He fed the stove.

"The draft is bad in here," she complained.

"I'll go to work on it. Didn't I say I would keep out the cold?"

He was a builder, a keeper of a lighthouse. He climbed up on the ladder to the third room's ceiling. Efficiently, he did God's bidding. He was a listener, too. At twenty-seven years of age, he sought in the woods to understand what he could from them. He did not understand his good mother's suffering a sinner's torments.

That blustery day he worked near her bed. Her face looks like a hawk's today, he thought. Her hands curled inside each other. She'd been this way for a month.

"The draft. Can you do something about it?" she begged.

"No, can *you* do something about it?" he asked her, impatient that she should feel the cold.

He strung a line. He was touched with grief. Outside, people wandered. Perhaps I have brought cold into the house with me, he thought. Perhaps *I* am tainted with cold and coming unto her high, holy bed a sinner.

For only a minute she was without a blanket, long enough for him to run the rope line from one corner of the new prayer cabin to the other corner. Then he strung another line. Gunnar positioned her on the bed to lie beneath where the ropes intersected. She was centered exactly where the lines met over her belly, precisely as far from one corner as another. In the process she'd been blessed by the cross the ropes formed. He gave thanks to the Lord. Perhaps because of the sign of the cross formed by the rope she would be getting better, he thought. Perhaps this cross was what she needed.

The thing—it was an owl, a snowy owl with wings five feet across when it flew.

Going out, Gunnar carefully pulled rags from the bottom of each door, but replaced them carelessly on the outside. No doubt drafts would come in, he thought, but in the woods he couldn't hear a complaint anyway. To get away from here, I can go as far as I choose, even out among the wolves and bobcats to learn of sin's cold, its grief.

With the moon nearly as bright as the night before, the cross on the roof threw its shadow from one bank of the river to the other. He made squares out of the moon's pattern on the snow. Kneeling in the center of the frozen river, he threw off his cap. One square held his coat; one his boots; one his cap; the last, his belt and gloves. Each square contained him no less than a minute before he retrieved his items from the treacherous snow. Paul watched him on the night of the eclipse; Paul, the owl who was an old, old man.

"What are you doing?" he'd said.

"Praying," Gunnar'd responded. "New prayers. Never-said-before prayers. Come here with me to the center of the square. These aren't conventional prayers."

"See how you've destroyed the shadows of the cross? I'm not sorry for you, Gunnar," Paul said.

After that, Gunnar'd gone home and driven his nails truer than before. Later that night, he knelt and prayed again that the snow and night make better sense to him. But Syl Magda called to him, interrupting his prayers.

Under the bright moon, Gunnar spotted the owl. It had been

on the roof for two days.

"Come down from there!" Gunnar hollered. "What do you want? No one's here that would concern you."

Atop the chimney, it fluttered. Gunnar was silent, the moon gone under when he closed the outer door.

Past midnight she started the hollering and banging. From the outer rooms he rushed to where she lay.

"What is it up there on the roof? What do I hear all the time?" she asked.

"There is no one up there," Gunnar said. "I saw no one."

"You saw—"

"I saw no one up there."

"You wouldn't notice my dark nature," his mother said. "Look at me, at my hands curling up. Please light a candle for me. Say prayers for my safekeeping. Purge me with hyssop, son."

"Mama."

"I'm cold on this raised and centered bed."

"I'll lower you."

"I know what he carries around his neck. See if he doesn't."

The light was dim. She complained to the crucifix over her bed. He prayed. She was silent, shaking.

"I can feel it," she said.

She was curling up on herself. Hands, arms, shoulders curling up.

"Father above," he prayed, "hear our plea," then he quit when he saw the owl's face in the window. Gunnar's mother thrashed about. He stoked the fire, bundled some furs over her. He went out of the shelter where she yelled from the elevated bed, went out, shut the inner door, opened the next, shut that, opened the next. Snow flew up. He edged around the corner. He was standing there facing Paul, who had the bag slung around his neck. Paul waved, gave the bag to Gunnar. The snow came between them, and he was gone.

Indoors, Syl Magda was still crying. She'd gotten so thin, so old. He loved her. He was like her more than anyone when he stepped into the prayer shelter again.

"You saw him, Gunnar. Please talk to me about him. I will choke on my words if you don't talk."

Gunnar was silent. When she started in this time, her voice was higher.

"I'm sick of the cold," she said.

"It's much warmer in here," he said.

She was talking about a coldness of sin he'd never felt.

"How did I know it was part of my nature to do as I did?" she said. "That man out there who's trying to get in, he got a speck of something—soot, dust—in his eye once."

"Yes."

"I leaned over him, licked his eye in the old country way."

"With your tongue you licked his eye."

"I did lick his eye."

"And I was a baby in my chair, you said?"

"Yes. And this was in Värmland and your father had set out to a mission place of dead souls. And this wasn't the one time I licked his owl's eye. I did this willingly. You in your chair I turned to the wall and hummed a melody to calm you while he waited in the room's shadows. He looked ancient when a pine knot burst and threw sparks around his feet. By then your father had been gone two months. Prayers to the Heavenly Father fell on deaf ears."

Gunnar rose up, took the cross from over her bed.

"I'm sick. I'm sick, dying. I can feel the cold, Gunnar. I'm full of sin's cold. Please pray and protect me, Gunnar."

"Please pray and protect you," he said.

He gathered the crucifix, the rope he'd made measurements with, some drawings. Syl Magda begged him not to take them away. She was weak, curled around the blankets.

"*I'm* sick," he said. "I'm the sick one."

In the window the face of a man whose fingers scratch away at perpetual frosts peered in. Gunnar saw from inside the room, could watch him right through the window. Gunnar carried the bag about his neck. There were the three of them in that desolate scene:

Gunnar, Gunnar's mother, and that cold and ancient master. She was wild. She didn't know where she was.

"Rest," he said.

She tossed her head from side to side. In the next room, he prayed. Not for her, but for himself. She appeared to twist in half. Bent up, old, she hollered for him.

"Son! Son!"

"Mother! Mother!"

He was praying hard. He read the sign in the window frost, the same sign he'd made in the river snow.

"We cut each other's hair. We kept it in the bag he's carrying. We did that," she said from the other room, "each time he came over. We talked about sin. We lay in the hair we'd cut off. When ice went out into the bay, my hair was on the table in Värmland. We'd cut it short. There was some power we shared by doing that. It wasn't good to lick his eye, Gunnar. I'm not sure what to think about it. I didn't know he died—now to show up, the dead man at my door. He reminds me of the coldness and treachery of sin."

"You're not sure what to think," Gunnar said. He himself was learning from the forest. He'd learned things out there. Because of his faith he was just learning. One thing was a new way to worship. *That is why—no longer alive to the warmth of prayer—spirits wander in death outside the window. Without warmth, without hope of light.*

He shut his eyes, tried not to shout when he opened the bag that hung around his neck.

"I'm dying!" she yelled.

"You're dying," he said.

"Cover me from the cold, Gunnar."

"Cover *me* from the cold, Mother."

He turned his head away and with a chair propped open the inner door. He kicked rags from the bottom, opened the next door, kicked those away, opened the next ... opened the entire shelter to the cold.

"Please help me," she said.

"Please help you," he said.

"I need some water now!"

"You need some water now."

He poured a cup from the dipper in the bucket. He dusted the surface with ash, handed her the cup.

"Thank you," she said.

"Yes. Thank me," he said.

In the other room, praying, he dressed for the forest cold. "*Jesu!*" he muttered on the way out.

Night trees caught his fur. He traveled through ash-dirtied snow to the gloomy places of the soul, observed others silhouetted against their fires. Gunnar saw the twilit sky.

She licked his eye when he had something in it. That was not the first time. Before father died, she consorted with souls whose cries now echo in the smoke-filled sky and hang like slate-gray ribbons from the trees.

Night and cold claim their own. But I am the truly sick one. For I renounce my building inward and my narrow rooms, a narrowness which I thought would provide. I renounce her—Syl Magda. And because now she begs in the midst of pleading for water and more covers, I throw off her blankets and salt her water with ash.

He went deeper, removing the wolves fur where the hazel brush had caught it. He was the keeper of the dead souls and the single light in the forest. He walked through their fires, dead men's fires unable to warm them, and knew he was their guide. Then he heard someone calling from deeper in yet, a man who looked like an owl.

"This way, Gunnar, here! You were teaching me down there on the river. Can you believe such a thing? That you were teaching me? Down on the river where the shadowy cross was—"

Gunnar removed his heavy gloves. Now there was no fire. No light whatsoever brightened his face. A fierce crying off somewhere in the wilderness.

"Here, this way, Gunnar, this way where we no longer have to listen to her futile beating against the cold."

AFTERWORD

I WAS OVERJOYED when editor and publisher C.W. Truesdale called in the summer of 1985 to say New Rivers Press would publish *Twelve Below Zero*. Although the stories had appeared in quarterlies in the United States and Canada, until then I'd not submitted a short story collection to a publisher. Twenty-three years and four other story collections later, I still rejoice when the stories I have struggled with will be collected in a new volume. Since the first *Twelve Below Zero* was published, I have realized more and more how grateful I am to many teachers—both for what I have learned from them and for the manner in which they've taught me.

My good fortune goes back more than fifty years to the Polish nuns at St. Adalbert's in Superior's East End. The sisters' influence in elementary school provides the backdrop for my life, although I will start this history of grateful thanks in a later year. By the time I was forty and by then had left Superior to attend graduate school at Brown University, to work on the East Coast, to resume graduate study at the University of Iowa, always returning home for lengthy periods, I still hadn't discovered the topic that would possess me as a writer—the ethnic character of a neighborhood, a church, and a Polish school. Not until my wife and I were leaving to teach at Northwestern State University in Natchitoches, Louisiana, and I feared I wouldn't be back for a long time did I compose a story about the passing of Polish ways in an old place.

Having read the piece in the first *Twelve Below Zero* (1986), Thomas Napierkowski, a professor of English at the University of Colorado-Colorado Springs, encouraged me in a review in *Naród Polski*, a Chicago Polish newspaper, to try more stories of Polish life. I have done so in the books since then. A constant teacher—constancy in the sense of loyalty, fidelity—Professor Napierkowski pointed me to the topic and setting I knew best, the Polish East End, though I hadn't realized the value of writing about the neighborhood. He has taught me other important lessons, as have many others.

When I submitted a version of my second book to Carl Brandt, the New York literary agent, he wrote that he preferred collections to be unified in tone, theme, and setting, whereas mine was in more of an anthology style. Good advice graciously offered by an important agent—and gratefully accepted by someone eager to write books. Professor Thomas Gladsky, then of Central Missouri State University, and the late Frederick Busch, then of Colgate University, continued my education. As I was following Mr. Brandt's advice, unifying *Children of Strangers*, Gladsky, who was writing *Princes, Peasants, and Other Polish Selves: Ethnicity in American Literature* (University of Massachusetts Press, 1992), warned me about filiopiety, ancestor worship. Having read the *Children of Strangers* manuscript, Frederick Busch, on the other hand, noticed a worrisome tendency toward too obvious author self-analysis in several of the stories, psychoanalysis masquerading as fiction. In recommending that Southern Methodist University Press publish the book, Busch cautioned my then-future editor, Kathryn Lang, "tell Bukoski [story writing] is about art, not about feeling better." George Garrett also recommended that the manuscript, after revision, be published.

Since then, Kathryn Lang, the most influential person in my writing life, has guided me through four books over sixteen years. Two of the manuscripts she rejected when I submitted them. A year later, after I'd reworked them and with the assent now of the presses' outside evaluators, she accepted *Polonaise* (1999) and *Time Between Trains* (2003), though another year's hard work remained before publication. Much earlier, *Children of Strangers* (1993)—and now *North of the Port* (2008)—required revision. Unwavering in her support, she has reminded me writing for publication is "a rough, tough game"—that there is no point in, nor resources for, publishing manuscripts that aren't ready to be published.

My writing "career," if I may call it so, owes primarily to Kathryn Lang, secondarily, as I say, to the many who have taught me: Professors Napierkowski, Gladsky, and Busch; Carl Brandt, who long ago wrote a kind letter; John Irving, who in his Spring 1975 Iowa Workshop class delighted in "Hello from Ture," giving me a boost when I was uncertain of myself; Ewa and James Thompson, Rice University, who recognize a glimmer of talent in the Polish American stories; and Barton Sutter, a well-published writer who, as a critic, shows extraordinary patience. Why does a person, after so many years, continue to care about another's work the way Barton Sutter has cared about mine? Reading my stories, he has forgotten his own interests in the desire to help me. (On other days, he helps his younger students.) Constancy. Steadfastness. How could I have managed without him, without any of these teachers? For all the help they've given, I hope the new, expanded *Twelve Below Zero* marks the work of a slightly wiser man.

Jim Perlman (editor and publisher of Holy Cow! Press) has provided the opportunity to make an old book new. The stories I have revised from the first edition (most of them written in Iowa City) reflect my passionate longing for the North. I am pleased to have had the chance, in the new edition, to reimagine this snowy country at the western terminus of the Great Lakes, where the wind, ice, and snow speak to you. Not only this, I have had an opportunity here to correct a misconception. To read my last four books, one would think the neighborhood of my youth was exclusively Polish when in fact many Swedes, Norwegians, and Finns lived there. Over the years I have appropriated the neighborhood, annexed it for Poland. Maybe now another writer can claim the East End I have held in trust for so long. With the 2008 *Twelve Below Zero*, I hereby return the neighborhood to the grandchildren and great-grandchildren of those other remarkable immigrants who have struggled physically far more than I have struggled intellectually with the hard land of northern Wisconsin.

Anthony Bukoski
Superior, Wisconsin
March 15, 2008

ABOUT THE AUTHOR

Born and raised in Superior, Wisconsin, where he lives with his wife, Anthony Bukoski joined the Marines in 1964 and, in 1965, served in Vietnam. Discharged two years later, he returned home to complete his baccalaureate. He then took an A.M. degree in English at Brown University; an M.F.A. degree in fiction writing at the Iowa Writer's Workshop; and finally, in 1984, a Ph.D. degree in English at Iowa. Along the way, he worked in the complaint department at a Sears store and as a short order cook, janitor, car wash attendant, and high school English teacher.

His stories have appeared in *New Letters, Quarterly West, The Literary Review, Image, Western Humanities Review,* and elsewhere and have been heard in live performance at Symphony Space in New York City, on National Public Radio's "Selected Shorts: A Celebration of the Short Story" program, and on Wisconsin Public Radio's "Chapter A Day" program. Bukoski's books have won awards from the Christopher Isherwood Foundation, the Polish Institute of Houston, the Council for Wisconsin Writers, and other organizations. His book *Time Between Trains* was a 2003 *Booklist* Editors' Choice. Since 1987, he has taught writing and literature at his alma mater, the University of Wisconsin-Superior.